C4

D0528575

..

....

....

....

....

....

....

....

Please retu
  shown abo
    be rene.

TEMPTED & TAMED

...by two red-hot men!

Meeting the hottest guys in town
changes the lives of sisters
Scarlett and Ruby Anderson for ever!

When sensible Scarlett is tempted by sinfully
sexy Jake—a doctor by day and a *sinner*
by night!—their one night of passion has
consequences that will last a lifetime...

And rebellious Ruby finally finds a reason to
stick around as deliciously hot racing car driver
Noah becomes the only man to tame her!

Be tempted and tamed by these red-hot heroes
in Emily Forbes's delectable duet:

A DOCTOR BY DAY...

and

TAMED BY THE RENEGADE

Both titles are available now!

Dear Reader

I'd like to introduce you to the Anderson sisters—Scarlett, Ruby and Rose—and their search for a happily-ever-after. Scarlett doesn't think she needs one, Ruby doesn't think she deserves one, and Rose looks as if she might not get one. But all that is about to change...

In A DOCTOR BY DAY... Scarlett—the rational, clever, eldest sister—is swept off her feet by Jake, a sexy younger man with an unconventional part-time job, who upends her orderly world and steals her heart. And in TAMED BY THE RENEGADE Ruby, the rebellious middle sister, falls in love for the first time when gorgeous Noah gets under her defences and teaches her how to love and accept—not only him, but also herself.

These two Anderson sisters might not have a lot in common, but I discovered they both have a thing for good-looking bare-chested men and, as usual, I had fun creating the heroes for my heroines. Jake and Noah are strong and loyal, smart and sexy, with slight non-conformist streaks—perfect for Scarlett and Ruby, even if they take some convincing.

I hope you enjoy these first two stories. I haven't decided if I'll give Rose her own story yet—she's putting up a good case for it in my imagination, but I'm tempted to let you decide. If you'd like to read about Rose I'd love to hear from you. Drop me a line at emilyforbes@internode.on.net

Until then, happy reading

Emily

Emily Forbes won a
2013 Australia Romantic Book of the Year Award
for her title
SYDNEY HARBOUR HOSPITAL: BELLA'S WISHLIST.

A DOCTOR BY DAY...

BY
EMILY FORBES

First published in Great Britain 2014
by Mills & Boon, an imprint of Harlequin (UK) Limited,
Eton House, 18-24 Paradise Road, Richmond, Surrey, TW9 1SR

© 2014 Emily Forbes

ISBN: 978-0-263-24400-7

Harlequin (UK) Limited's policy is to use papers that are natural,
renewable and recyclable products and made from wood grown in
sustainable forests. The logging and manufacturing processes conform
to the legal environmental regulations of the country of origin.

Printed and bound in Great Britain
by CPI Antony Rowe, Chippenham, Wiltshire

Emily Forbes began her writing life as a partnership between two sisters who are both passionate bibliophiles. As a team, 'Emily' had ten books published. One of her proudest moments was winning the 2013 Australia Romantic Book of the Year Award for SYDNEY HARBOUR HOSPITAL: BELLA'S WISHLIST.

While Emily's love of writing remains as strong as ever, the demands of life with young families have recently made it difficult to work on stories together. But rather than give up her dream Emily now writes solo. The challenges may be different, but the reward of having a book published is still as sweet as ever.

Whether as a team or as an individual, Emily hopes to keep bringing stories to her readers. Her inspiration comes from everywhere, and stories she hears while travelling, at mothers' lunches, in the media and in her other career as a physiotherapist all get embellished with a large dose of imagination until they develop a life of their own.

If you would like to get in touch with Emily you can e-mail her at emilyforbes@internode.on.net

Recent titles by Emily Forbes:

THE HONOURABLE ARMY DOC
DARE SHE DATE THE CELEBRITY DOC?
BREAKING THE PLAYBOY'S RULES
SYDNEY HARBOUR HOSPITAL: BELLA'S WISHLIST*
GEORGIE'S BIG GREEK WEDDING?
BREAKING HER NO-DATES RULE
NAVY OFFICER TO FAMILY MAN
DR DROP-DEAD-GORGEOUS
THE PLAYBOY FIREFIGHTER'S PROPOSAL

Sydney Harbour Hospital

These books are also available in eBook format from www.millsandboon.co.uk

Dedication

For romance readers everywhere,
this book is written as a thank-you to anyone
who has ever read one of my stories.

I started writing this story just after
I won the Australian Romantic Book of the Year award for
SYDNEY HARBOUR HOSPITAL: BELLA'S WISHLIST.

I was thrilled and honoured to win a RuBY,
which is a reader-voted award,
and I definitely couldn't have done it without your support.

I hope you enjoy this book too, and in particular Jake.
He is my gift to you!

Love, Emily

CHAPTER ONE

'LET ME GET this straight. Richard proposed and you turned him down?'

Scarlett turned and leant in close to her friend's ear, taking care to avoid the spiky tips of Mel's short pixie haircut. 'Shh,' she whispered. 'I don't want everyone to know and I'm sure Richard doesn't either.'

Mel's voice hadn't been overly loud but this wasn't a conversation Scarlett wanted the rest of the girls in their party to hear. She worked with most of them and she didn't want to be the subject of rampant hospital gossip and she certainly didn't want to be the one to start a tale.

She flicked a glance over their group but most of the girls seemed to be more focused on getting inside the club than listening to her and Mel. Candice, the bride-to-be, was at the front of the line, the long white veil she wore making it obvious she was the hen on the hen's night. The veil was longer than her dress and Scarlett thought she looked ridiculous but what would she know, hen's nights were not really her thing.

Neither was fashion, she thought as she wriggled her toes, trying to encourage some circulation into her extremities. Her feet were killing her. She'd borrowed a pair of platform stilettos to team with her simple black dress. The shoes and her make-up were the only concessions she'd made to dressing up for the night out but the strappy sandals were proving to be a big mistake.

Scarlett's taste in clothing tended towards timeless classics, she wasn't a trend follower. It was a waste of good money, in her opinion, and her feet were now reminding her of her momentary lapse of reason. She couldn't wait to get inside and sit down. The short walk from the restaurant in Leigh Street to the Hindley Street club was about her limit in five-inch heels.

She couldn't believe she was keen to get into the club. Spending an evening at a male revue, especially one called The Coop, wasn't something she had ever done before and she could only imagine what the experience would be like—although if the guy on the door was any example she wasn't going to need to rely on her imagination.

Candice's name was on the door, allowing them to bypass the queue and giving them free entry. Apparently Candice knew someone who worked here and Scarlett wondered where on earth you'd meet someone who worked in a strip club, but as the cute young shirtless guy on the door ushered them inside she decided she didn't care, all she wanted was to sit down.

'I want to hear all about it once we're inside,' Mel said, as another buffed and shirtless male greeted them and led them to their table. The club was dimly lit and it took Scarlett's eyes some time to adjust to the lighting. A T-shaped stage jutted out into the centre of the club, the catwalk stretching into the tables that were clustered around the stage. A mirrored bar lined the far wall and a dance floor hugged the back wall and was already packed with young women dancing and singing. The noise level was high and almost unpleasant, but Scarlett hoped that might work in her favour. Perhaps the noise would make any sort of conversation impossible.

She followed the girls to their table, which was front and centre at the end of the catwalk, and sank into a chair. Jugs of bright green cocktails were delivered, promptly poured into glasses and passed around, and Mel waited only until everyone had a drink before she continued her interrogation.

'So Richard was lying in his hospital bed, recovering from heart surgery, working up the nerve to propose, and then you knocked him back?' she asked, as she sipped her drink. It seemed Scarlett wasn't going to get out of this.

'It wasn't like that,' Scarlett protested. Surely Mel couldn't believe she'd be that heartless.

'Don't tell me he was down on one knee beside his bed?'

'No.' Scarlett shook her head. 'He was out of hospital.'

'Well, that makes all the difference,' Mel teased. 'How did he take it when you said no?'

Scarlett could tell Mel was enjoying her discomfort but she had made her decision for what she knew were perfectly valid reasons and she wasn't going to marry the guy just because he'd had a mid-life revelation.

'He was okay. What other choice did he have really? It was my decision. He can't change my mind. I think marriage is overrated and it's not for me.'

'Don't let Candice hear you.'

'She already knows. Richard showed her the ring he bought me, he wanted her opinion.'

'He bought you a ring!?'

Scarlett nodded.

'What was it like?' Mel's curiosity took another turn.

'Gorgeous,' she admitted. And it had been. A square-cut solitaire, over one carat in size, set in platinum. It was in a traditional setting and was exactly right for her, classic and expensive. 'Almost gorgeous enough that I wanted to accept his proposal.'

'So why did you say no?'

'I was thinking about saying yes but then he started talking about having kids and I freaked out. I don't want kids.'

'Really? How come I never knew that?'

Scarlett and Mel had been friends for years, since meeting on the first day of med school, but Scarlett hadn't realised she'd never shared her feelings about children. She supposed the topic had never come up before now.

'Kids are a huge sacrifice. Believe me, I should know. I've seen what my mother gave up to raise me and my sisters. I've worked really hard to get to this point in my career and I'm not done yet. I'm not going to give it all up to raise a family.'

Scarlett could feel the effects of the cocktails they'd been drinking on top of the wine she'd had at dinner. She could hear her words weren't as crisp as usual, a bit blurred around the edges, a bit of a lisp on the essess. She knew the alcohol had loosened her tongue too. She wasn't normally so forthcoming about her personal life but she and Mel had shared a lot over the years since they'd been paired as lab partners on their first day at uni. They had been the only two who hadn't already known someone—Mel had moved to Adelaide from Tasmania and Scarlett had been a mature entrant.

She'd felt years older than everyone else and hadn't been used to the social nuances of teenagers, even though she'd only just been out of her teens herself.

Their isolation had been the only thing they'd had in common initially but they'd both recognised that it hadn't mattered. Over the years their friendship had grown until Mel felt, in a lot of ways, like another one of Scarlett's sisters, only a lot less trouble.

'But you don't have to have kids right now,' Mel countered. 'It could wait until you've finished your final exams.'

'I'd still need to establish myself in anaesthetics before I could take time off and Richard doesn't want to wait. He's forty-three and he's just had a major health scare. It's made him reassess his future.' Richard's recent heart attack and minor surgery had been a big shock to him at a relatively young age and Scarlett knew that coming face to face with his own mortality had been the trigger for his proposal and his reassessment of his priorities.

'You could get a nanny. And a housekeeper. The two of you could afford to pay for whatever help you want.'

'So I get married, have babies and then hire a nanny and a housekeeper.'

'Sounds all right to me.' Mel grinned.

Scarlett shook her head. 'Having or not having kids wasn't my only reason for turning him down. It just didn't feel right. It was more than just his desire to have a family. When he proposed it should have felt like a moment I'd been waiting for my whole life, but I remembered being more excited about getting accepted into my anaesthetics specialty than receiving a marriage proposal, and surely that's wrong. My heart was racing, but not with excitement, I think it was panic. There was no impending sense that this was the next stage of my life and I couldn't wait for it to get started. I could have married him but it would have been for the wrong reasons. At the end of the day, I didn't love him enough.'

She also knew that she'd been scared. Terrified even. She didn't want to have children with someone so much older and who had heart problems. What if he died and left her a single mother? That was exactly what had happened to her own mother and it was not what she wanted in her own future. She didn't love Richard enough to take that chance. It was easier to let him go.

She had thought Richard would be a safe choice, she'd thought he wanted the same things as her. She'd thought his focus was on his career and that because he was already in his forties he wouldn't want children. Wouldn't he have had them by now if that was the case? But when things had turned out differently from what she'd expected, she'd discovered that she didn't love him enough to change her mind. She didn't love him enough to risk everything she'd worked for.

'So that's it. All over?'

'It's the right decision. I know it is. I'm not even sure he loves me either. I think a lot of his plan for the future was driven by timing and circumstances and not so much by his love for me. He had never mentioned wanting children before his heart attack. I think he'd be marrying me for the wrong reasons too.'

Scarlett picked up her cocktail glass. The wait staff was well trained and had obviously been told to make the most of the break in the entertainment to keep the drinks coming. No sooner had one jug been emptied than another was delivered. Scarlett sipped her drink. She didn't really need more but she wanted to let the alcohol numb her a little bit. She didn't want to spend the night thinking about Richard. That chapter of her life was over and she wasn't planning on having any regrets.

She'd been working and studying hard since she was sixteen and she had a few more years to go. She wanted to finish her studies and she wanted time to enjoy the fruits of her labour. She didn't want to be tied down at the moment. Surely that was a sign she wasn't ready for marriage. Surely that was a sign that it was time to have some fun.

'Let's talk about something else. I'm moving forward with my life, starting tonight.'

She looked around at all the women who were getting into the spirit of the evening, not just at Candice's table but throughout the room. She got the feeling she could let her hair down and not be judged. There was a sense of *what happened in the strip club stayed in the strip club* feel to the night. Maybe it was the effect of the green cocktails but Scarlett decided it was time to join the party.

Another round of cocktails had just been brought to their table and this time it was Scarlett who refilled their glasses before she turned her attention to the entertainment. Another set had just begun and the stripper on stage was young and athletic and, in her uneducated opinion, very good at his job. She felt slightly uncomfortable appreciating the 'talent' of the much younger men on stage but considering she was hardly the oldest female in the room, and she was certainly not the loudest in voicing her appreciation, she decided she would be rude not to enjoy the show.

By the time the set came to a close the green hue of the drink was starting to make her feel a bit nauseous. She wasn't used to drinking much, her job didn't really allow for it, and she knew if she didn't make sure to drink some water she'd regret it in the morning.

'I think I need something other than alcohol,' she told Mel. 'I'm going to the bar. Do you want anything?'

Mel shook her head as Scarlett pushed her chair back and stood up, pleased to find she could feel her toes again after resting her feet. She picked her way through the tables, dodging the good-looking, scantily clad waiting staff. She didn't want to make eye contact with them but there didn't seem to be any other polite place to look as she made her way across the room.

The bar staff was all cut from the same cloth as the waiters. They were all men, all shirtless and all cute. Not one of them had any chest hair or any body fat. They were all waxed and tanned and gorgeous and Scarlett gave them each a quick once-over before they had time to notice her.

The barman closest to her was slicing lemons. He was about three feet away and standing in profile to her. He had a sculpted jaw, small ears and brown hair, cut shorter at the sides and longer on top, that he'd obviously run some product through with his fingers to keep it spiked up. The deejay was playing a faster-tempo dance number now and all the barmen were moving to the music. Nothing choreographed, their movements looked natural and Scarlett wondered if they even knew they were dancing. She watched his hips as he kept time to the beat. His abdominal muscles flexed as he twisted to reach another lemon, drawing her attention away from his butt. His skin was smooth and tanned and his triceps tensed as he slid the knife through the flesh.

He finished dissecting the last lemon and scraped the slices into a bowl, using the back of the knife. He slid the cutting board into a sink as he twirled the knife through his fingers. Scarlett held her breath and watched as the light reflected off the blade. She gasped as he lost control of the knife and it left his hand and spun through the air. She watched it fall and waited for it to hit the floor, waited for it to stab into something it shouldn't.

It landed on the floor behind the barman, where it lay innocuously on the rubber matting. No harm, no foul, but he'd heard her gasp and before he retrieved the knife he turned to look at her. He grinned. A cheeky, quick smile that lit up his face and made Scarlett think he made a habit of mucking around and that he didn't mind getting caught.

He held her gaze and winked at her. Scarlett blushed and quickly broke eye contact but when, out of the corner of her eye, she saw him turn around to pick up the knife she automatically went back for a second look. His jeans had stretched firmly across his butt and Scarlett couldn't help but admire him. His buttocks were round and firm and the denim of his pants moulded perfectly to his backside.

She was still looking as he stood up and turned to face her, catching her by surprise. Her blush deepened and she couldn't pretend she hadn't been checking him out but luckily he didn't seem offended if his broad grin was anything to go by. He didn't seem to mind being stared at but, then, why should he? He was gorgeous and probably very used to it. She didn't imagine she was the first woman to have been caught perving on him.

He ran the knife under hot water and put it to one side. He grabbed a tea towel to dry his hands and then tucked the towel into the waistband of his jeans. Scarlett's eyes followed his movements. His jeans were loose at his hips and as he shoved the tea towel under his waistband the movement pushed his jeans even lower, giving her a glimpse of the diagonal line of his inguinal ligament. When she realised what she was doing she quickly raised her eyes, only to find he was still watching her.

He took three steps and came to a stop in front of her. He was still grinning and Scarlett was flustered, unsettled and unsure where to look.

'What can I get you?' he asked.

His voice was deep but quiet and she found herself leaning towards him as she tried to hear what he was saying. They were separated only by a few inches now and his features came into sharp relief, almost as though he'd been projected onto a glass pane in front of her. His green eyes were deep set and as he looked at her it seemed he could see what she was thinking.

His bottom lip was full even while he was smiling and his nose was perfectly straight, flaring slightly at the bottom into a small triangle. His chin and jaw were shaped like the bottom of a flawlessly proportioned pentagon and the angles of his face gave him an almost perfectly symmetrical appearance. His tanned shoulders were dusted with freckles and his jaw was lightly stubbled, and at close range he looked older than she'd first thought. But he was still young, mid-twenties maybe, definitely younger than her. Not that his age mattered. Sure, he was cute and his body was divine and he certainly looked like he would know how to show a woman a good time, but it was irrelevant to her.

Sexy young strip-club barmen were not her thing, even if they did have the ability to disconnect her brain and make her struggle to speak. He was waiting patiently for her answer and if he could read her thoughts, as she suspected, he was no doubt amused by her lack of reply.

'May I have a glass of water, please?' she managed

to ask, just as if it looked like he was about to repeat his question.

Her words sounded strange and she could feel her tongue sticking to the roof of her mouth but she wasn't a hundred per cent sure it was from the alcohol. It could also be because of the half-naked man standing in front of her. She'd seen plenty of naked or semi-naked bodies before but it wasn't every day that one as fine as this appeared before her. Was it any wonder she was struggling to think clearly, let alone speak?

He turned and scooped ice into a glass with his left hand and Scarlett caught a glimpse of a tattoo on the inside of his left biceps, several inky black marks making a dark impression against his skin. He turned to pick up a slice of lemon from the bowl he'd just filled, obscuring his tattoo from view. He dropped the lemon onto the ice and grinned at her as it hit the cubes. His hips kept time with the music as he filled the glass with water and Scarlett's stomach did a peculiar flip as she watched. He looked completely comfortable in his skin and there was something very sensual about his movements.

'Anything else I can do for you?' he asked, as he placed the glass on the bar. His eyes swept over her face, from her eyes to her lips and down to her chest as he spoke to her. Scarlett knew the neck on her dress was high enough that there was no hint of cleavage but she blushed as if she was the one standing there half-naked, not him. His swift gaze was practised, she had no doubt he had plenty of experience at giving women a quick once over, but even she could see the appreciation in his eyes. She could feel her pulse beating between her thighs, and she could feel it getting stronger as the heat in his gaze intensified.

She swallowed and reached for the glass, only to find he hadn't let go of it yet. Her fingers touched his and a surge of electricity shot through her. She snatched her hand back as if the glass was hot instead of filled with ice-cold water.

He was smiling at her again as he pushed the glass closer before removing his hand. His green eyes laughed at her but not unkindly as he asked, 'First time?'

She looked at him in mute surprise. There was no room in her head for conversation as unfamiliar hormones ran rampant through her bloodstream.

'I'd remember if I'd seen you before,' he added, and Scarlett wondered if the bar staff relied on tips. That would explain why he was being so friendly.

But water was free, wasn't it? There was no need to tip and, therefore, no need for him to flirt with her. She'd never had a stranger flirt with her. She wasn't really the type. She knew it was because she never encouraged eye contact, she didn't have the knack of catching or holding someone's attention. She knew the barman had only noticed her because she'd gasped when he'd dropped the knife and she was positive he was only flirting with her out of habit.

She glanced around, partly to confirm that he was actually talking to her and partly to see if anyone was paying them any attention. The bar area wasn't busy; most of the women seemed happy to utilise the club's table service and let the shirtless waiters come to them. The focus of the room was the stage and the tables were set facing that way, which meant most of the women had their backs to the bar. No one was looking at her. No one except the hot barman.

She wasn't sure what she should do in this situation but, since no one was watching her and to ignore him would be rude, she smiled back. 'You have women who come here often enough that you can recognise them?'

'Believe it or not, we get a lot of regulars. Birthday parties and hen's nights are good for repeat business. We've even had repeat customers who hold divorce parties.'

'Divorce parties?'

'The club owner thinks divorcees are an untapped market. Cashed-up women looking for some fun.' He shrugged his smooth, sculpted shoulders. 'He's right and they do seem to enjoy themselves but I take it that's not why you're here?'

She shook her head and replied. 'Hen's night.'

Her eyes flicked across the room to the group she'd come with. No one seemed to have missed her and while she felt as though time was standing still she'd probably only been gone from the table for a few minutes.

As she scanned the room the stage lights came on and started pulsating. The deejay started spinning a eighties disco number and the dance floor cleared as everyone made their way back to their seats and focussed their attention on the front of the room as the next act, an athletic stripper in a sailor's outfit, took to the stage. Scarlett could see the stage from the bar. It was in the club's interest to make sure all patrons had a good view, but she wasn't in any hurry to return to her seat, she was more than happy with the view she had here. She checked again but it seemed as though her absence wasn't being noted. She guessed her company couldn't compete with a semi-naked man gyrating on a stage.

'You're with Candice?' he asked. Apparently he had followed her line of sight.

Scarlett's eyes shot back. 'You know her?' she asked,

as she remembered that Candice had known someone who worked here. Was this him?

'We're old family friends,' he explained. He pulled the tea towel from the waistband of his jeans and began wiping the bar. It was already spotless and Scarlett wondered if it was a delaying tactic. Was he delaying so he could talk to her? A warm glow spread through her. She couldn't deny she was enjoying the attention. 'Do the two of you work together?' he asked.

Scarlett nodded.

'Are you a nurse too?'

She shook her head. 'I'm a doctor.'

Her answer surprised him. He'd thought he was a good judge of character and while he didn't think she looked like a nurse she looked even less like a doctor. Her neck was long and slender, her face a perfect oval. Her lips were full and pouty, shiny with a pale pink gloss. In contrast, her eyes were dark and mesmerising. Outlined with kohl, the lids dusted with dark eye shadow and her lashes coated with mascara, her eyes looked as though they could have a thousand secrets hidden in their depths.

Her hair, a brown so deep it was almost black, was thick and she'd pulled it back into a bun at the nape of her neck. His fingers itched to reach across the bar and pull the pins out, to let her hair cascade over her shoulders.

He realised it was the bun that had thrown his judgement off. It was far too severe for her stunning features and gave her the appearance of someone who worked in administration. All she needed to complete the look was a pair of glasses.

On the surface she looked like organised efficiency but his imagination suggested that underneath the surface was a different story. Perhaps he'd been working at the club for too long, he thought as his mind wandered. Maybe he was having difficulty separating fact from fiction, reality from fantasy.

'What's so funny?' she asked.

He shook his head as he realised he was smiling. 'Nothing.' She was a doctor who worked with Candice. It wasn't funny, it was perfect, but the story would keep for another day. 'I'd better get back to work. Tell Candice I'll come over later and say hi.'

He watched as she left the bar and crossed the room to return to her table. He wasn't in a hurry to get back to work—checking her out was far more interesting. Her body was smoking hot. She had poured it into a simple black dress—round neck, sleeveless, zipped down the back. He wondered if she was trying to disguise her assets, but the sway of her hips drew his attention to her narrow waist and round bottom. He was enjoying watching her walk away.

Her dress stopped just above her knees and his eyes travelled lower. Her legs were bare, no stockings, and her calves were pale, her ankles slender. She was wearing heels, ridiculously high heels, which might explain the sexy sway of her hips. He just had time to notice her shoes had a leopardskin pattern before she slid into her seat at the end of the catwalk and the stage hid her legs from view.

He was fascinated. Her swollen lips, mysterious eyes, generous D bust and her unexpected shoes all contrasted sharply with her no-nonsense hairstyle and plain dress. She was a bombshell disguised as a secretary. Which part of her was real? Was she even aware of the bombshell? Was her outfit smoke and mirrors or did she really not know how hot she was? Did she ever let the bombshell out and how could he arrange to be there if she did?

By the time she sat down at her table, Evan, the sailor stripper, had been replaced by Caesar, a muscular man of Fijian descent, who was clad only in a loincloth. The guys were warming the crowd up again with their routines. As Jake mixed a fresh batch of cocktails Caesar backflipped off the catwalk and began dancing through the crowd, looking for a willing participant for his act. Jake watched Candice's friend as he measured and poured. He could see she was trying to avoid eye contact with Caesar, desperate not to be picked and dragged into the spotlight. Just watching her made him grin. She was definitely a club virgin.

He watched as she dipped her head to the side, bringing him into her line of sight. She saw him watching her, a reversal of their earlier roles, but not one to be embarrassed at being caught out, he gave her another wink.

Scarlett felt herself blush again. What was wrong with her? Why couldn't she keep her eyes to herself? Why did she keep seeking him out? She'd just turned down a marriage proposal and yet her head was full of lustful thoughts about a complete stranger.

She tried to focus instead on the dancer, *stripper*— she wasn't sure what they called themselves—only to find that his act was finishing and his spot was being taken by another man, slightly older than the others but just as buff and tanned, who wore tight black leather pants and nothing else. He held a microphone and greeted the audience in a loud, showman's voice, 'Good evening, chicks, and welcome to The Coop.'

'Good evening, Rooster!' A chorus of women's voices split the air as the majority of the audience called out a greeting in return.

'Listen up, ladies, the Himbo Limbo is about to begin. Choose your competitor and send them to me,' he said, as he spread his arms wide in an expansive, all-encompassing gesture that made the muscles on his chest and arms ripple.

'I nominate Scarlett!' Candice shouted, as she bounced in her chair.

Scarlett frowned. She had no idea who this Rooster character was or what he was talking about. 'What on earth is a Himbo Limbo?' she asked.

CHAPTER TWO

'IT'S JUST A limbo competition,' Candice told her, 'with a twist.'

Scarlett felt her antennae twitch. She could sense a disaster in the making or at the very least some embarrassment. 'What sort of twist?'

'The "Himbo" part refers to two strippers. Instead of using poles, the Himbos hold the rope,' Candice explained.

That didn't sound nearly as risqué as Scarlett's imagination had led her to envisage but she couldn't understand why Candice was sending her up if it was all so tame. 'Why don't you do it?' she asked, as Rooster called for the nominated hens or chicks to come forward.

'You do yoga, you should be flexible,' Candice replied, 'and, besides, I can't limbo in this skirt, it doesn't leave much to the imagination when I'm standing up straight, let alone if I'm horizontal.'

Scarlett couldn't argue with that, Candice's skirt was incredibly short. She didn't know if she was any more suitably attired, her little black dress was hardly limbo-appropriate, but regular yoga classes meant she was reasonably flexible so maybe it wouldn't be all bad. She hadn't expected games but it was highly likely there

would be more embarrassing contests to come and this
sounded like it could be one of the lesser evils.

She glanced around the room. Most of the tables
seemed to be nominating a participant, although the
majority seemed to be brides-to-be, not 'chicks'. She
finally clicked why the club was named The Coop—
it was full of hens and chicks and one very loud and
proud Rooster.

'C'mon, Scarlett, do it for me, it'll be fun,' Candice
pleaded.

Scarlett thought it would be about as much fun as
getting her legs waxed but she wasn't sure how she
could get out of it. It was unlike her to put herself in
the spotlight but as the girls continued to egg her on she
found herself giving in. Maybe she'd had one too many
cocktails, she thought as she said, 'All right, I'll do it.'

Just as she stood up the two 'Himbos' appeared
front and centre on the floor beside the catwalk. Scarlett breathed a sigh of relief. At least it seemed as though
she wouldn't have to actually get up on the stage. The
men were both very toned, no surprises there, and
dressed in what could only be described as very tiny,
very snug leather shorts. Scarlett thought one of the
men was the stripper who had just finished his routine.
He had swapped his loincloth for white shorts, which
were a sharp contrast to his dark skin but left nothing
to the imagination.

The other 'Himbo' was in a pair of slightly more
respectable black leather shorts. Scarlett had never
thought she'd consider men wearing tiny leather shorts
'respectable' but it seemed as though there was a fair
bit about tonight that was going to challenge her traditional and conservative views.

Just when she thought it was safe to join in, the Himbos sprang up onto the stage and Rooster called to the girls, 'Okay, hens and chicks, make your way up to me.'

A spotlight swept the room and came to rest on the gaggle of women gathered by the stage before it moved to illuminate a short flight of stairs leading up onto the catwalk. Scarlett was horrified to realise they were expected on the stage after all but slightly mollified by the sight of the stairs. It was a relief to know they weren't expected to spring onto the stage in the Himbos' footsteps—she certainly wouldn't be springing anywhere in her borrowed platform heels.

The women made a beeline for the steps, eager to get the competition under way, as Scarlett held back. The steps had no railing and she didn't want to get jostled and go sprawling up the stairs in front of everyone. She was going to be embarrassed soon enough just doing the limbo, she didn't need to start by making a complete fool out of herself.

The women clustered around the Himbos as the deejay played dance music. The women and the Himbos were all dancing, with the exception of Scarlett, who tried her best to blend into the background behind the others, although that was hard to do given she was almost five feet eleven inches tall in her five-inch heels. Fortunately Rooster began to introduce the Himbos to the audience, which Scarlett took to mean that the contest would be starting soon and she wouldn't have to be embarrassed for too much longer. The Fijian stripper in the short white shorts, Caesar, was introduced first, followed by Rico, who was introduced as the 'Italian Stallion'. The audience cheered and clapped as the Himbos took their places.

'And now I'd like to introduce our judge for this evening,' Rooster crowed, somehow managing, through sheer force of personality, to keep the attention on himself. 'A favourite among the chicks, our very own Judge Jake.'

The cheers of the audience turned into wolf whistles and the noise in the club reached maximum volume as Candice's friend, the barman Scarlett had been talking to earlier, came up onto the stage. It seemed she wasn't the only one who thought he was delicious.

He had changed his outfit but Scarlett was happy to see he wasn't wearing leather pants—she'd seen enough leather pants tonight to last her a lifetime. He'd changed from regular denim jeans into a black pair, which hugged his thighs. His chest was still bare and he had a length of rope looped over one shoulder and slung across his torso. He jogged across the stage, moving lightly and waving to his adoring audience, and Scarlett's level of embarrassment increased with every step he took towards her. It was too late to back out now but she wished the stage would open up and swallow her. She tried in vain to hide, even though she knew it was futile. He was going to see her standing there sooner or later.

Caesar and Rico had stepped in front of the women, creating some space, and Jake passed them each a black strap, which they fixed around their chests. At the front of the strap, positioned over their sternums, was a hook that looked like a mountaineering karabiner. Jake hoisted the rope from his shoulder and handed it to the Himbos. At each end of the rope was a small metal loop, which Caesar and Rico clipped into the karabiners.

Scarlett's eyes widened in surprise. She hadn't expected the rope to be tied around their chests, she'd expected them to hold it, stretched out between them. That would have given the competitors plenty of space to move but once the rope was tied around their chests and clipped into the karabiners it was quite short and didn't leave a lot of room to manoeuvre. Not, Scarlett thought, that most of the girls would mind, but she had no intention of brushing against half-naked strangers any more than she had to.

Jake waited until the limbo rope was in position before taking the microphone from Rooster and taking over the contest. The girls were asked to line up and after much jostling Scarlett found herself third in line behind two hens, one rather large one and one with an exceptionally long veil. Judge Jake approached each competitor in turn and asked them their name. He showed no surprise when he got to Scarlett and she knew then he'd already seen her on the stage. She just hoped he didn't think she'd volunteered.

Even in her heels she was still an inch or two shorter than him, and she had to look up slightly when she told him her name. Up close she could see that his green eyes were ringed with brown and he winked at her as he repeated her name and Scarlett felt her cheeks redden. She hoped the tell-tale blush wouldn't be noticeable but she suspected the spotlight would only serve to enhance the colour in her face.

With much cheering and clapping from the audience Jake got the contest under way. The plump hen went first and she could almost walk under the rope without ducking, she was so short. The next hen, the one with the long veil, wasn't so lucky. She trod on her veil as she tipped her head backwards to duck under the rope. This pulled her up short and made her fall and she landed hard on her backside. Her faux pas was greeted with laughter from the audience, though not cruel or nasty laughter. Scarlett knew most of them would be laughing with relief that they weren't the ones lying flat on their backs in front of a crowd.

She couldn't work out how the hen had managed to trip herself up but as she was sprawled on the floor and Jake was reaching for her hand to help her to her feet Scarlett just prayed that she wouldn't be as unlucky or as ungainly. She was next in line.

'How confident are you?' Jake asked her, as she moved a step closer.

Scarlett looked at the girls around her, including the one already disqualified. 'I've done a few limbos in my time,' she fibbed. 'I think I can take this one.' Her knees felt weak and she wondered how she was going to manage to limbo on wobbly legs but her voice sounded surprisingly normal and strong.

She wasn't sure why she'd chosen to announce her lies to the room; she could only assume it had something to do with the challenge in Jake's eyes. She didn't want to look like a complete klutz in front of him but neither did she want to appear timid and pathetic. She didn't normally think of herself as a competitive, win-at-all-costs type of person but she didn't like to fail at anything. She had high expectations of herself and she certainly didn't want to be beaten by these women.

Jake laughed and announced, 'Scarlett Take-No-Prisoners, who is standing in for her hen, Candice, let's see what you've got.'

The girls on her table whooped and cheered as Scarlett easily limboed under the rope and popped up on the other side.

After Scarlett were another six competitors, four hens, one with a rather heavy, awkward-looking tiara holding her veil in place, and two chicks. Two more fell on the first attempt and Scarlett thought the success rate was probably indirectly proportionate to the amount each 'chick' had had to drink.

As the contest continued and the number of competitors dropped, so did the height of the rope. As the rope descended the Himbos shortened it too, bringing them even closer together and giving the chicks less margin for error. Another two stumbled and were eliminated as the rope was lowered to the bottom of the Himbos' rib cages.

The girls were being urged on by their friends but despite the encouragement all but two were out of the competition after attempting to limbo under the rope when it was level with the Himbos' waists. By the time the rope was moved further south to their hips Scarlett's until-now-unknown competitive streak had well and truly emerged and she had no intention of losing tonight. It was now a two-chick race between her and a girl named Tracey and it was Scarlett's turn.

Scarlett sized up the competition. Tracey was several inches shorter than her so Scarlett slid her platform heels from her feet to level the playing field. The rope was very low now and she didn't need to make this any harder than it already was.

'Watch out, Tracey.' Jake laughed. 'The competition is getting serious, clothing is being shed. What else is coming off, Scarlett?'

His green eyes were challenging her again and something in his expression made her want to challenge him back. 'Nothing yet,' she quipped, and was rewarded with a brief spark of something—maybe attraction, maybe anticipation, she wasn't sure—but there was definitely a light in his eyes. She turned her back, wanting to leave him hanging, and shimmied under the rope. She just managed to scrape under without over-balancing.

Jake had stepped around to the other side of the Himbos and was there to take her hand as she straightened. He kept his elbow bent, which kept her close, and his hand warmed her skin where it wrapped around her fingers. He smelt clean, as if he was freshly showered but she knew that couldn't be the case. He smelt good.

She could feel the heat coming off his half-naked body and she knew the skin on his chest would feel as warm and soft as his hand. Scarlett's stomach trembled as Jake continued to hold her hand as they waited for Tracey to take her turn at the limbo. Her body was tingling as Jake's touch awakened her senses and she could feel the pulse low in her belly starting to beat a little bit faster.

Scarlett knew she could pull her hand out of Jake's grasp but she didn't want to. This connection would be severed soon enough and she wanted to enjoy it while it lasted. They watched as Tracey almost made it under the rope before falling at the last hurdle, putting her hand on the ground just before she was ready to stand and thereby disqualifying herself.

Jake let go of Scarlett to help Tracey to her feet. 'I'm sorry, Tracey, you almost did it,' he said as he helped her up, before turning back to Scarlett. 'That makes you our winner tonight.' His smile lit up his green eyes as he added, 'Would you like to see how low you can go?'

Scarlett watched as Caesar and Rico moved the rope down another couple of inches until it was sitting across their groins. She looked back at Jake. He was now grinning mischievously and she knew he was waiting to see if she was up to the next challenge. She shook her head. She'd let him win this round. 'I'm done.'

'All right, here's your prize.' Jake reached his left hand behind him and when he brought it forward again

he had a handful of fake money that he must have had
stashed in his pocket. Scarlett frowned. What was she
supposed to do with fake dollar bills?

He held the notes up in the air and Scarlett got another glimpse of the tattoo on the soft side of his arm. At
close range she could see that the inky black marks were
stars, five of them in total, their arrangement making
a pattern that was familiar to every Australian. He had
the Southern Cross constellation tattooed on his skin.

Jake kept his arm held high as he turned through one
hundred and eighty degrees, showing the fake money
to the crowd, who cheered as he called out, 'Tipping
dollars!'

'Tipping dollars?' Scarlett repeated. She had no idea
what he was talking about.

Jake lowered the microphone and leant in close as
he pressed the fake banknotes into her hand. 'It's to tip
the dancers,' he explained. 'Tuck some into the guys'
shorts before you leave the stage and share the rest with
your group for them to use later.'

The crowd applauded and cheered again as she
tipped the Himbos while Jake escorted Tracey from
the stage, but before she could follow the crowd began
to chant, 'Jake, Jake, Jake!' and she knew she was expected to tip him too. She wasn't certain but she thought
Candice might have been leading the call.

Jake was back by her side again. He didn't seem surprised or reticent and she suspected he loved the attention. She'd bet his star sign was Leo. They loved the
limelight. She tucked a few notes into his waistband and
as her fingers brushed against his hipbone she found
herself searching his skin for more tattoos. But the skin
of his torso and waist was smooth, tanned and ink-free.
Her heart was hammering in her chest and she could

feel a blush stealing across her cheeks. Somehow touching Jake felt a lot more personal than when she'd been
tipping Caesar and Rico.

With shaky hands she picked up her shoes and fled
the stage, retreating to the relative safety of her table.

'That was a side of you I hadn't seen before,' Mel
said as she sat down.

'And don't expect to see it again any time soon,'
Scarlett replied. Her heart was still racing, making her
sound breathless. She hoped everyone would think it
was from the exertion of the limbo, although she knew
it was a reaction to Jake.

Performing in front of a crowd was completely out of
character for her but part of her had enjoyed the chance
to pretend to be someone else, someone less worried
about behaving appropriately and less concerned about
being who people expected her to be. Perhaps it was a
case of 'anything goes' tonight or maybe normal inap-
propriate behaviour was considered appropriate within
the four walls of The Coop, but she didn't have time to
consider it any further as Mel interrupted her musings.

'I thought it was rather entertaining. But, tell me,
who is Judge Jake and how does he know Candice?'
Mel asked, as Scarlett handed the remaining tipping
dollars to Candice.

'We're old family friends,' Candice interrupted. 'He's
coming over now, I'll introduce you.'

Scarlett turned her head. Sure enough, Jake was ap-
proaching their table. He was no longer bare-chested,
he'd put on a black T-shirt and a black leather jacket
but, if anything, he looked even better. No, not better,
she thought, but just as good.

Candice made quick introductions before Jake
grabbed an empty chair from the table beside theirs.

He flipped it around with a practised move and wedged it in between Scarlett and Mel before straddling it backwards. His long legs stuck out sideways and brushed against Scarlett's thigh.

'So you do own a shirt,' Scarlett said, as her eyes raked his torso.

'And a jacket,' he teased.

He was leaning forward over the back of the chair, his arms crossed. The teasing note in his voice and the gleam in his eye made her feel bold. She reached out and ran her hand down his sleeve. 'There's a definite leather theme going on in this place.'

'Hey,' he said, as he sat up straight in the chair, held the jacket on each side of the zip and lifted it slightly, adjusting it on his shoulders, 'this is mine.'

'It's nice.' It was. She could smell the leathery fragrance. She hadn't noticed a leather smell on the Himbos, not that she'd got that close to their shorts.

'Yeah?'

She grinned, feeling more at ease. It was much less stressful now she was out of the spotlight and off the stage. 'Much better than leather pants.'

'Have you ever worn leather pants?'

Scarlett shook her head.

'Well, you should give them a go, you might be surprised at how comfortable they are.'

'You have leather pants too?'

He raised one hand. 'Guilty as charged. Call it part of our uniform. But you might be pleased to know I don't own leather shorts.'

'That's a relief,' she said, but, as much as she thought leather was being worn a little too often around the club, she suspected he would look rather good in leather pants. She suspected he'd look good in anything.

He shifted in his seat and his thigh brushed against hers for the second time. Her nerve endings sparked and it felt as if all the cells in her thigh muscles were straining to get closer to him, as though they were trying to leap out of her skin. She moved her leg away from his before she could be tempted to lean into him instead.

The alcohol she'd drunk tonight had most certainly reduced her inhibitions. Not only had she voluntarily got up on stage, she was now having lustful thoughts about a complete stranger. She was planning on having fun but she wasn't sure if her courage stretched far enough to include Jake. She should go home before she did something even more out of character. Before she could be tempted by a cute young barman who might, or might not, be flirting with her. There was no way she was going to make a move on him, well, not the first move anyway. She needed to get out of here. If he wanted to come with her that was his choice. If he chose to stay behind then she'd assume she'd read the signals wrong. There was a good possibility of that, she thought. She was hardly the most experienced woman at the table.

She'd done her duty to Candice. Surely she could leave now without appearing rude. She leant across the table to speak to Candice, ready to make her excuses. 'I think I might head off, if you don't mind. I had a really busy night on call before working today.'

'How are you getting home?'

'I'll take a cab.'

'Do you want me to come with you?' Mel asked. 'You shouldn't go on your own.' Hindley Street was not the street you wanted to walk down alone.

'I'll wait with you, if you like,' Jake said to her. 'I've finished my shift and was about to go anyway.'

'Perfect! Thanks, Jake.' Candice agreed on Scarlett's behalf without any hesitation. 'That way, Mel can stay and enjoy the rest of the evening. You don't mind, do you?' Candice asked, as she looked at her.

Scarlett didn't want to be accused of breaking up the party so she did what came naturally to her and agreed. 'Sure,' she replied. She'd had a lifetime of experience at being the one to keep the peace, being the one to do what everyone expected of her while her sisters did as they pleased, so of course she agreed, but it didn't hurt that she was more than happy for Jake to keep her company. She knew then that his touch had been deliberate and the thought sent a frisson of excitement through her body.

'Jake is one of the good guys, you can trust him,' Candice added, before she turned to Mel and whispered with a chuckle, 'I'm not denying he could charm a nun out of her habit but that's Scarlett's good fortune.'

As Scarlett ducked her head under the table to put her shoes back on and search for her handbag she heard Candice say something about charm but she couldn't catch the whole sentence. She thought about asking her to repeat her comment but when she found her handbag and looked up she saw that Jake was standing, ready to pull out her chair for her. Not wanting to keep him waiting, she decided that if what Candice had said was important she'd find out some other time.

She followed Jake from the club, aware of several women checking him out as he passed their tables, but their attention was short-lived as another dancer was on the stage and now that Jake was fully clothed there were obviously more interesting things to look at elsewhere. Scarlett didn't mind, she was happy to have him all to herself.

There was a taxi rank opposite the club but the queue was horrendously long, stretching for half a block. Knowing it could take for ever for her turn to come, she released Jake from his obligation. 'It's going to take ages, you don't need to wait,' she said, as they joined the end of the queue.

'I promised Candice I'd look after you.'

'That's okay, I won't tell her.' She smiled. 'Thank you for offering but it's busy enough. I'll be all right,' she said, as she slipped her shoes off. Her feet had had enough and she couldn't stand the thought of another minute standing in uncomfortable high heels. The concrete pavement was rough but cool under her skin and was soothing in an unexpected way. She glanced down the line and saw she wasn't the only one who'd divested herself of her footwear.

'Come on, I'll give you a lift,' he said, looking at her bare feet.

'It's fine, really,' Scarlett insisted. 'I'm just not used to wearing high heels.'

'I'm not going to leave you here and I think we've both got better things to do than stand on the street for an hour.'

His tone wasn't impatient. Maybe she was reading things into his words but the depth of his voice and the low volume made it sound as though the better things he had in mind involved them both and she was tempted to dive in, recklessly, heedlessly, and accept his offer. But her natural inclination not to cause trouble made her ask, 'What if I live miles away?'

'Then that's my problem. I'm not going to retract my offer. I'd look like a jerk.'

She looked up at him. Barefoot, she was now several

inches shorter than he was. 'I'd hate to have that hanging over my head.'

'So, can I drop you home?' He grinned and all her objections, few though they were, vanished. She nodded and slipped her sandals back on before following him as he retraced their footsteps.

He led her to an alleyway behind The Coop and Scarlett followed blindly. She knew she would feel unsafe if he wasn't beside her but even though he was virtually a stranger she trusted him. It was an odd situation to be in, she wasn't normally a trusting person, particularly not when it came to men, but she only got good vibes from Jake and he wasn't really a stranger, was he? He knew Candice.

He stopped beside a dark green convertible that had been parked behind a dumpster, which kept it partially shielded from view. The roof was down and there was a cumbersome, heavy steering lock clamped to the wheel.

Jake opened the passenger door and shrugged out of his leather jacket. 'Here,' he said, as he held it out to her. 'It might be a bit cool with the top down but it's a bit temperamental and it'll be quicker and warmer if you wear this.'

Scarlett slipped her arms into the sleeves as Jake held it for her. His fingers brushed her neck as he turned up the collar. The jacket was much too large for her but it was warm and smelt divine, a heady combination of leather and clean male. She didn't bother to zip it, just pulled it close, wrapping it around her like a cocoon.

She sank into the low seat as Jake stowed the steering lock behind them and started the engine. The sound was low and throaty and reminded her of his voice. Scarlett relaxed. She closed her eyes and let the warmth and scent of the leather of the seats and Jake's jacket seduce her. It was nice to have someone else make a decision for her. Not being required to think was a novelty. All her life she had been the one people turned to for advice. She had been the one who everyone relied on to be sensible, responsible, to make the hard decisions, and Scarlett's natural tendency was to carefully consider all angles before making an informed and logical choice.

Letting a stranger give her a lift home was not the sort of thing she did. She wasn't a spontaneous sort of person. Every decision she made was carefully measured, considered and weighed before she acted on it. She was used to being in control. Of her life and of her actions.

Going home with someone she'd just met was the sort of thing her sister Ruby would do. Ruby would have set her sights on a guy the minute she walked into The Coop and wouldn't have thought twice about letting them give her a lift home. Even their younger sister, Rose, was more outgoing than she herself was. She would have walked into The Coop, tossed her blond hair, batted her long eyelashes and her big blue eyes and within minutes she would have had men falling at her feet. She would have flirted expertly and at the end of the night she would have been spoilt for choice if she wanted a lift home.

Scarlett didn't know if she could ever be as confident or as fearless as her sisters but it was kind of nice to step out of her comfort zone for a change. But she knew the only reason she felt safe to do that was because there was a connection with Jake. She wasn't thinking about the physical or chemical connection she felt but rather the safer, more reliable one that was their common friend, Candice. Scarlett knew that no matter how gorgeous and charming a man was, she would never let a complete stranger give her a lift home. She just didn't do things like that.

'Scarlett?'

She jumped as she felt Jake's hand on her knee. She opened her eyes to find they had left Hindley Street behind. The little green car was on the bridge over the River Torrens as Jake headed up Montefiore Hill.

'Are you okay?' he asked, and she realised he must have been speaking to her while she was daydreaming.

'Yes. I'm fine.'

Jake flicked the indicator on to turn at the lookout at the top of the hill. She tried not to notice the cars parked there, certain that the occupants were up to no good as they looked across the city lights. She had never fooled around in the backseat of a car but sitting here with Jake's hand still resting on her knee she could almost imagine what it would be like. But he removed his hand to negotiate the corner, leaving a cold circle the size of his palm on her skin. He drove past the old cathedral and up towards O'Connell Street.

'Are you hungry?' he asked, as the car idled at the next set of traffic lights.

'I am,' she said, as she rubbed at the cold spot on her knee. She was a little surprised to find she was hungry but dinner seemed like hours ago.

'My favourite late-night take-away is just up here. We can grab something to eat there, if you like?'

'Sure.' She thought it was probably a good idea to eat something else and soak up the rest of the alcohol she'd consumed but where they ate was another decision she was happy to let Jake make.

Jake slowed his sports car as they approached the café strip and he searched for a parking space. A car was pulling out from the kerb and he waited, taking the spot in front of a café with distinctive blue-and-white signage. She recognised the café; she'd walked past it plenty of times but had never been inside, but it seemed that Jake knew it well.

'Jake, how's it going?' The guy behind the counter greeted him as they walked in. 'What'll you have, the usual?'

'Sounds good,' he said, before explaining to Scarlett, 'You can't go past George's lamb yiros,' he told her.

There was a huge selection of dishes written on the blackboard above the counter but Scarlett could see the lamb revolving slowly on the enormous spit, cooking as it turned, and the smell carried to her. It smelt fantastic. She'd never tried a yiros before but it was an easy decision. She nodded. 'Make that two,' she told George.

'You want garlic sauce with that?' George asked.

That sounded rather potent and Scarlett wasn't at all familiar with yiros etiquette. Jake was watching her, his head tipped to one side, waiting for her answer. She didn't want to be in close proximity to him if she had garlic sauce and he didn't. Even in a convertible she suspected it could be unpleasant.

'Is that how you usually have it?' she asked Jake.

'Yep.'

'Okay, then.' Scarlett watched as George expertly carved slices of lamb as it rotated on the spit and piled it onto flatbreads and garnished it with garlic sauce and salad before wrapping each yiros in wax paper and handing them over the counter. She followed Jake to a table tucked into the back corner of the café. All around them other patrons were devouring their yiros but from what she could see it was almost impossible to eat daintily. Worried about making a mess of Jake's jacket, she slipped it off and hung it over the back of her chair.

'Do you want to take your shoes off too?' Jake was smiling at her.

She shook her head. 'Not in here.'

'You could take them off on the street, why not in here?' he said, as he tore the wax paper to expose the top half of his yiros.

'We're in a restaurant. Earlier I couldn't face the thought of standing any longer but I'm okay as long as I'm sitting down,' Scarlett said, copying his actions.

'I've never understood why women insist on buying uncomfortable shoes—although they do look great on you.'

'Thank you.' The compliment almost made the pain worthwhile. 'But they're not mine and I didn't realise they were so uncomfortable. I borrowed them,' she admitted. 'Strip clubs aren't really my scene and I don't own anything suitable to wear to one.' She took a bite of the warm flatbread. The lamb was tender and juicy, perfectly complemented by the sauce.

'Going to the club doesn't mean you need to dress like a stripper.' He laughed.

She stuck one foot out from underneath the table, pointing her toes and swinging her foot from side to side. 'You think these look like stripper shoes?'

Jake raised one eyebrow and grinned. 'That wasn't what I meant,' he protested.

'I wonder what my sister would have to say about that!'

Scarlett smiled back before taking another bite of her yiros, only to discover a fraction too late why she should have said no to the garlic sauce as it squirted out of the bread and ran down the side of her hand. She was holding the yiros with two hands, trying to stop it from falling apart, and there was nothing she could do about the sauce that was now running over her wrist and heading for her elbow.

Jake reached across and ran his finger along her forearm, wiping the sauce from her skin. He was watching her as he put his finger in his mouth and sucked the sauce from it and Scarlett felt as though he'd run his tongue along her bare skin. She could see the heat in his eyes and could still feel the heat from his finger as it sent a current shooting through her.

'You've got sauce just here too,' Jake said, and Scarlett held her breath as he stretched his hand out and wiped the side of her cheek. His thumb grazed the corner of her lip and Scarlett couldn't help it—her lips parted under his touch and it was all she could do not to capture his thumb with her mouth. She inhaled deeply as Jake removed his hand and this time wiped his fingers on his serviette.

Despite the fact that they were sitting in a busy café, surrounded by other people, she was aware only of Jake. She ate the rest of her yiros in silence, acutely aware of him sitting opposite her, but somehow she managed to finish eating without any further mishap.

She felt the first wave of fatigue roll over her as she wiped a serviette over her lips and stifled a yawn.

'Are you ready to go?' Jake asked.

She was tired but in no hurry to get home. She was quite happy to sit for a bit longer in his company but she had no reason to delay. She stood as Jake picked his jacket up from her chair and slung it around her shoulders. He left his hand around her back, holding the jacket in place as he walked her to his car. Scarlett had to squeeze in close to him to manoeuvre between the tables and chairs and she could feel the length of his body where he pressed against her. The night air was cool on her skin when he released her to open the car door and she pulled his jacket more tightly around her to make up for the loss of warmth.

Within minutes she had directed Jake to her house. The night was over.

Almost.

Jake was out of the car and was walking her to her door.

'Thanks for the lift,' Scarlett said, as she unlocked her front door.

'It was my pleasure.' He was leaning on the doorjamb, watching her quietly.

'And for supper,' she added, reluctant for the evening to end.

Light spilled from the hallway and fell on Jake, illuminating him where he stood. She was in shadow but she could see Jake's hand reaching towards her shoulder.

'What are you doing?'

'Something I've been wanting to do all night.'

He was leaning forward. Was he going to kiss her? His head was next to hers, his lips beside her ear, and his voice was quiet and deep. She could feel the gentle puff of his breath on her skin as he spoke and then she could feel his fingers in her hair as he pulled the end of her ponytail and untucked her hair from its bun. He pulled her hair forward and loosened it over her shoulders and his hands brushed her skin.

'That's much better.'

Scarlett turned her head and lifted it, just slightly, less than an inch, to look at him. He was still watching her and the way he looked at her made the heat pool low in her belly. She could feel a fluttering of nerves, a tremble in her stomach, but the nerves were anticipatory, not anxious. Jake's green eyes were shining emerald in the light. His lips were millimetres from hers. He dipped his head into the shadow and closed the gap. His lips were warm and hungry, soft yet demanding. His body was lean and hard and his hands on her arms were firm but gentle. Scarlett pressed herself into him as two of them became one.

His hands slid behind her, cupping her bottom, holding her to him.

She wound her hands behind his head as her lips parted in response to the pressure of his tongue.

She was standing on her front porch, kissing a stranger, but he didn't feel like a stranger. Scarlett felt as though she belonged with him, as though she'd known him always. Every cell in her body responded to his touch. Every part of her recognised him, as though they'd met before, and as she kissed him she felt as if she was reuniting with a lover, not making out with a stranger.

She brought her hands to his chest and placed them flat against his pectoral muscles. She grabbed a fistful of his T-shirt, bunching the fabric up in her palms, and dragged him out of the doorway and into her hall.

She should be saying good-night. She should be thanking him for the lift and saying goodbye but the look in his eye and the taste of his mouth had disengaged her brain and she couldn't let him go. Not yet. She knew their first kiss was only a taste of what was to come.

She stepped to her right, towards her bedroom door, and her lips left Jake's mouth. He was watching her closely, his green eyes intense, and she knew he was waiting to see what she would do next. She knew it was her decision now.

She pushed the front door closed and stepped backwards into her bedroom.

Jake didn't wait for an invitation. He stepped towards her, following her lead. His hands were behind her back and she felt him slide the zip on the back of her dress down and her dress fell at her feet. She stepped out of it, naked except for her underwear and her borrowed heels.

The light from the hallway penetrated the darkness of her room. Scarlett stood still as Jake ran his gaze over her. He dropped his head and kissed her neck. Scarlett arched her back as his fingers trailed after his mouth.

Jake whipped his T-shirt over his head and suddenly there was bare skin on bare skin.

He scooped her up and laid her on her bed.

She bent her knee and slipped a finger under the strap at the back of her sandal.

Jake felt her movement, sensed what she was doing. 'Leave them on.'

Scarlett dropped her hand and let her knee fall as Jake ran his fingers from the inside of her ankle, up her calf to the inside of her knee. His fingers left a line of heat behind and Scarlett felt herself melt at his touch. Her eyes drifted closed.

'Scarlett?'

She opened her eyes. 'Hmm?'

'How much have you had to drink?'

His question startled her. 'Why?'

'I want to be sure I'm not taking advantage of you,' he said, as his hand continued to move higher, to the soft, warm junction at the top of her thigh. He was watching her, waiting for her to stop him, but she couldn't. She was melting in a pool of desire.

'You're not,' she told him. 'I know what I'm doing.'

She actually had no idea what she was doing—this

was completely out of character for her—but he didn't know that. He didn't know the real Scarlett. He didn't know that she was normally in control of her actions and emotions. As far as he knew, she went out every weekend and drank cocktails and danced until dawn. For once, maybe it would be fun to be that girl. She wasn't hurting anybody and she could use some fun.

She wanted to lose herself in his touch. She wanted to lose herself in his embrace. She didn't want to think, she didn't want to make decisions. She wanted Jake to take her away from reality. She would worry about tomorrow another day.

Tonight she intended to take what she wanted and tonight she wanted Jake.

CHAPTER THREE

SCARLETT STRUGGLED OUT of bed on Monday morning. She felt unaccustomedly lazy after an indulgent and unusual weekend and it took twenty minutes of yoga and two cups of coffee before she was ready to face the day. Her stint in Emergency was still ongoing and she knew she needed to be focused and sharp while working there, but she was having trouble keeping her attention on what had to be done. Her mind kept wandering off to relive the events of Saturday night.

If she closed her eyes she could picture Jake lying naked and almost exhausted in her bed. They may have only spent a few hours together but she knew she'd always be able to recall the ridges of his abdominal muscles and how they'd felt under his fingers, how his green eyes had lit up when he'd laughed and how it had felt making love to a fit, young and flexible male. It had been quite an experience.

She'd never slept with anyone with a tattoo before; she'd never slept with anyone she'd just met before and never on a first date. They hadn't even had a date—she couldn't count the late-night yiros stop at the café. She still couldn't believe she'd slept with him.

She grabbed a third coffee from the kiosk on her way into the hospital, wondering if she'd have time to drink it and knowing she probably shouldn't. Two cups was probably enough for now. The triage nurse solved her dilemma for her.

'Can you go straight into treatment room three?' she said, as she confiscated Scarlett's coffee and waited for her to sign in for her shift. 'We have a fresh lot of med students and one of them has asked for an anaesthetic consult.'

All day yesterday she'd imagined being someone else, someone more like Ruby, someone who acted spontaneously and did crazy things without regard for others. But one night of rebellion did not make her Ruby. Ruby was the fun sister, Rose was the pretty one, Scarlett was the clever one, and that was the way it had always been. And now she was a doctor and with that hard-earned qualification came certain responsibilities, which included an ability to focus and concentrate. She took a deep breath and shook her head to clear the last of the weekend cobwebs from her mind as she pulled back the curtain and stepped into the treatment room.

There were three people in the cubicle. A blond-haired, angelic-looking toddler, about two years old, was sitting on her mother's lap, cradled in her arms. The mother's face was white, the daughter's face was tear-streaked, and sterile dressings had been draped over her left hand.

The doctor sat opposite the pair and looked up as Scarlett stepped into the space. As their eyes met Scarlett felt as though all the air in her lungs had been knocked out of her. The doctor was the spitting image of Jake. The same green eyes, the same chiselled jaw. The similarity was uncanny.

She knew she was staring but she couldn't seem to stop.

'Hello, Scarlett.' It was the same voice. The same cheeky grin.

'Jake?' There was a stethoscope poking out of his coat pocket, a white doctor's coat. None of this made sense. 'What are you doing here?'

'I'm here on a uni placement.'

'You're a med student?'

'Yep. And this is Margie and her daughter, Skye.' With those few words Jake got Scarlett's attention back on track. She had a job to do, she'd have to deal with the issue of his appearance later.

'Skye managed to grab hold of some exposed live wires on the back of an old electric heater this morning. Luckily she was wearing sheepskin slippers with rubber soles but she sustained third-degree burns to several fingers. She's going to need surgery but I need an opinion as to whether a wrist or arm block would suffice or whether she'll need a GA.'

'How old is Skye?' Scarlett asked Margie, as she took two steps across the room to the basin to wash her hands.

'Twenty-six months.'

'And has she ever had an anaesthetic before?'

'No.' Margie shook her head.

'Let me see the extent of what we're dealing with.' Now that Jake had told her what had happened Scarlett was aware of the odour of burnt flesh but she still wasn't prepared for the state of Skye's fingers.

Jake lifted the dressings and Scarlett noted that he only lifted the side closest to her, keeping the injury shielded from Margie and Skye. The skin on Skye's middle, ring and little fingers was badly burnt. Charred and black, and Scarlett wondered if they'd be able to save them.

'The flesh will need debriding at the very least and most likely she will need plastic surgery. She'll need to be kept very still and that would be an impossibility for a two-year-old, so she'll need a general. I'll book a theatre.'

Scarlett was in a hurry to escape the cubicle. The space was far too small for her and Jake. She couldn't breathe and she knew it wasn't the smell of burnt flesh that was affecting her. It was Jake.

She knew she needed to ignore him. She knew it was better to treat Saturday night exactly as what it had been—a once-in-a-lifetime abjuration of character. It wasn't something she planned to make a habit of and while she couldn't deny she'd enjoyed the experience, a man like Jake didn't fit into her plans. Not even short term. He wasn't her type. He was sexy and fun and she knew she wasn't either of those things.

She gave instructions to the triage nurse and went to change. She was pleased she was going to be busy. She'd worry about Jake later.

She hurried into Theatre, pulling up short when she saw a familiar figure fiddling with the MP3 dock in the corner. Richard was back at work.

Damn. How on earth could she have forgotten his sick leave was finished and that he was returning today?

She knew it was because her head had been filled with thoughts of Jake, so much so that everything else had been wiped from her mind. Added to that, the surprise of seeing Jake again this morning had completely obliterated any chance of her remembering anything else. Guilt burned inside her as she waited for Richard to turn around. She could feel her cheeks flush and her palms were damp with sweat.

Why did it have to be today? She wasn't prepared for this, not now.

She took a few deep breaths as she tried to quell her guilty feelings. She hadn't done anything wrong, and there was no reason to feel guilty. Her business was no longer Richard's business and there was no need for him to know what she'd been up to.

He turned around as their patient was wheeled into Theatre and Scarlett's heart sank as she saw Candice and Mel on either side of the barouche. She prayed they would keep tight-lipped about the events of Saturday night.

The usual flurry of activity—transferring the patient to the operating table and beginning sedation as Mel, who was a plastics registrar, discussed the surgery with Richard—meant there was no time for idle conversation, but as soon as everything was set Candice's first question let Scarlett know she wasn't going to be so lucky.

'Did you get home all right on Saturday?' Candice asked, as she covered their patient with sterile drapes. The tone of her voice made Scarlett suspect she knew more than she was letting on but, judging by the expression on her face, she didn't seem to be hiding anything, although Scarlett was terrified that Candice was going to say more. Candice was an experienced nurse and she was quite capable of continuing a lengthy and detailed conversation while she worked.

'Yes.' She kept her answer short. She didn't want to get into this in front of Richard.

'What did you do on Saturday?' Richard asked, as he prepared to begin putting their patient back together.

'It was my hen's night,' Candice replied.

Scarlett did not want to open a discussion about Saturday night's activities so before Richard could ask any more questions she tried to steer the conversation towards Richard's health instead. He had been off work for several weeks and it would be rude of them not to enquire as to how he was feeling. She glanced at Mel, hoping she would pick up the conversation.

Scarlett felt like a wanton woman. Her behaviour on Saturday night had been completely out of character and even though no one in the room had actually witnessed it, she still felt like everyone could see on her face what she'd been up to. She'd had casual sex with a stranger or, at best, a new acquaintance, only weeks after dumping her boyfriend, who had wanted to become her fiancé and was now standing two feet from her across an operating table. Even though she was entitled to behave as she pleased, the guilt she was experiencing only emphasised the fact she was ill equipped to be acting so out of character. She was far better suited to being responsible and careful and considerate. Being spontaneous might be all right for Ruby but it obviously didn't suit her nature. She needed to remember that.

She let her thoughts drift as she heard Mel take over the conversation. Richard's MP3 was playing in the background. He liked to listen to instrumental versions of bands like Dire Straits and The Police and today it was the Adelaide Symphony's performance of Queen's songs. Scarlett would normally hum along but her mind was elsewhere.

She'd made a mistake. But she'd learn from that. She didn't plan on repeating her error.

She knew she couldn't do casual. She couldn't live in the moment. The moments always seemed to follow her. She didn't know how Ruby did it. How did she go from one man to the next without blinking an eye?

She herself had a tendency to dwell on things, which was why she tried to do the right thing in the first place. She hated feeling guilty or feeling like she'd done wrong, which was exactly how she felt right now, not because she hadn't enjoyed herself but simply because it was so out of character for her. She wasn't like Ruby and she wasn't like her youngest sister Rose either, where she could breeze through life without a care in the world, not minding what other people thought of her. Scarlett didn't want to be judged unless she knew she was going to be judged favourably and she doubted that would be the case if people knew about Jake.

The sounds of Theatre continued to flow around her as she monitored her patient's condition until finally the surgery was finished. Scarlett reversed the anaesthetic and left the patient to be taken through to Recovery.

'Is everything all right?' Candice had followed Scarlett into the scrub room. Scarlett thought about asking her why she hadn't mentioned that Jake would be turning up at work today but she thought better of it. She didn't want to invite questions.

'Of course,' she replied, as she threw her gloves, cap and mask into the rubbish. 'Why?'

'You barely said a word during the whole procedure. Is Richard making things awkward for you?'

'No.' Scarlett shook her head and it was only then that she realised Richard had barely spoken to her. Had he been giving her the cold shoulder or had he been concentrating on the surgery? She had no idea. But she realised she didn't care. Not at all. Working in silence was preferable to making idle conversation at the moment. She had a terrible poker face and she didn't trust herself not to give away her guilty feelings. 'I'd forgotten Richard was coming back to work today. I hadn't prepared myself for that and it threw me off a little.'

It wasn't completely true. Seeing Richard had thrown her but not because he was back at work—it had only bothered her because of her guilt but she wasn't about to air her dirty laundry here. The fewer people who knew about her indiscretion the better. 'I need a coffee,' she told Candice. 'Are you coming?'

Candice shook her head. 'Not yet. I need to go into Recovery first.'

Scarlett was relieved. She didn't want company, she needed a moment of solitude. She walked through Emergency. The department was busy. Most of the curtains were pulled and people hurried to and fro. Scarlett was grateful to find the tearoom empty. She made another coffee and grabbed a biscuit. She stood by the window with her back to the door. She really needed something more substantial to eat. Her stomach was in turmoil; all the coffee was making her edgy and her nerves were already fraught, but the solitude of the tearoom was more appealing at the moment than braving the cafeteria crowds.

She heard the door open and she half turned her head, more a reflex than anything, to see who was interrupting her peace and quiet. She hoped it wasn't someone who felt like talking. The door opened fully and Jake walked in.

He winked at her. She couldn't believe how confident and cheeky he was, but the combination obviously served him well—it had worked on her. Her knees were shaking and she leant against the window, gripping the ledge with one hand to stop herself from collapsing to the floor. She wanted to touch him, to make sure he was real. She desperately needed to find some self-control.

If she wasn't holding on to the window sill she knew she'd probably be halfway across the room by now.

She *never* reacted like this and her reaction irritated her and made her cranky. 'Have you come to tell me why you kept this news to yourself?'

'What news?' he asked, still grinning. 'That I was a med student or that I was coming here?'

'Either. Both.' She couldn't think straight.

'Would it have mattered?'

'Yes.' There was no way she would have jumped into bed with someone who would be turning up at her workplace virtually the next day.

'You never asked what I did.'

'I assumed you worked in a bar.' Scarlett was unsettled.

'You thought that was *all* I did?'

Scarlett shrugged. 'I guess.' He was right. She hadn't asked if he did anything else. She hadn't actually given it much thought. She hadn't wanted to know too much about him. She'd wanted it to be anonymous but she was annoyed with him for saying nothing. Confusion and guilt were making her short-tempered. 'You knew I worked here, you obviously knew on Saturday night that you'd be here today, and you still said nothing.' She felt as though he'd tricked her.

'I didn't think it mattered.'

'It matters to me.'

She felt like a fool. This was why she should never make spur-of-the-moment decisions.

Why hadn't he told her? Why hadn't *Candice* told her?

'Did Candice know you were going to be doing a placement with us?' she asked.

'Yep.'

'Why didn't she tell me?'

'Why would she think you cared?'

He had a point. And Scarlett didn't have an answer. 'What is the problem?'

Where did she start? How did she explain it? Would he understand that Saturday night had been completely out of character for her? Would he understand that her lapse in judgement had risked everything she'd worked so hard for?

It was unlikely. She couldn't expect him to understand.

He crossed the room, coming to stand beside her. She glanced nervously at the door. There was no telling how long their privacy would last. 'This isn't the place for this conversation.'

'No, I suppose it's not. It wasn't my intention to make things awkward, so for that I apologise. Why don't we have a drink together tonight and you can tell me why it matters and I can apologise properly?'

She didn't care about an apology. What she did care about was her reputation. And sleeping with a tattooed med student who worked in a strip club was not the way to get ahead in her career. It was not the way she wanted to catch people's attention. No matter how sexy he was.

Now that she'd recovered from the shock of seeing him, she was able to study him more closely. He was clean-shaven today. His face was all smooth angles and his green eyes had a look of amused interest. He was wearing a crisp white shirt under his white coat and he looked, and smelt, clean and fresh. And young.

He dipped his hand into the pocket of his coat and pulled out a container of breath mints. He offered them to her and when she shook her head he tipped a couple into his hand. Scarlett followed his movements. The mints were tiny against his large palm but it was his long, delicate fingers that caught her attention. She could remember how they had felt on her skin. The pleasure he'd brought her with his touch. It was a shame to think that one night was all she could have but there was no alternative. She had plans that didn't include sexy young male students.

'How about The Botanic at eight?' he suggested. Apparently his plans differed from hers.

'No.' Scarlett gave a slight shake of her head. The Botanic was much too close to the hospital, they would have no privacy there. There were plenty of other pubs in the two kilometres between the hospital and her house and any number of bars in Rundle Street.

Why was she even considering other pubs? Her response simply should have been 'No' and that was that. She could think of half a dozen reasons why she shouldn't meet him but only one why she should. And that reason was enough to have her thinking of alternatives. She needed a chance to make her position clear. He was likely to be on placement in her hospital for the next month and she needed to lay down some ground rules.

The door to the tearoom was opening again and Scarlett had to make a quick decision if she didn't want to risk being overheard. 'How about The Queen's Head?' she proposed, just as Candice appeared.

'Jake! You're here.' Candice bounced over and hugged him and Scarlett took the opportunity to escape from the tearoom while Jake was otherwise occupied. But before she could leave he held up eight fingers— *eight o'clock*—behind Candice's back and nodded at her in silent confirmation of their date.

Only it wasn't a date and Scarlett chose her outfit

very carefully to ensure there would be no way Jake could misconstrue the purpose of their meeting. She chose a navy suit jacket and matching pencil skirt. She put a simple white silk camisole under the jacket and pulled out court shoes with a small heel, nothing as ridiculous as the platform sandals she had worn the night she'd met him, and redid her hair, pulling her thick curls into a tight bun. She needed a barrier of power dressing; she hoped it would combat their chemistry.

She spotted him the moment she walked through the front door into the bar. He was in the room to her right, leaning against the bar, keeping an eye on the entrance, waiting for her. God, he was gorgeous.

She was right on time; he'd obviously got there early. She wondered if he'd done it deliberately. And, if so, had it been so she didn't have the upper hand or was he just being chivalrous, not wanting her to wait alone at a bar?

He was wearing jeans and a white T-shirt with a green surf logo on the front that matched his eyes. The stark contrast in the formality of their outfits didn't go unnoticed by Scarlett and she was struck again by their age difference. But it wasn't enough to wipe out the instant surge of attraction she felt when their eyes met. She was aware of other women casting their eye over him as well. He exuded sex appeal and she wasn't the only one to notice, although he seemed completely unaware of the attention.

He straightened up and took two steps across the room, meeting her halfway. He leant towards her and kissed her cheek.

A surge of desire and adrenalin rushed through her and her body threatened to betray her. This was going to be harder than she'd anticipated.

'You came,' he said, as he let go of her hand and straightened up.

Scarlett wondered if he'd really doubted her. She'd bet he'd never been stood up by a woman.

'What would you like to drink?' he asked, as she re-sisted the urge to put her fingers over the spot on her cheek where she could still feel the imprint of his lips.

'A glass of wine, please.'

'Shall we share a bottle?'

She shook her head and reminded herself to be strong, decisive. *Remember, he must only be about twenty-three*, she told herself. *Just deal with him the same way you deal with Ruby and Rose. Firmly and de-cisively.* Scarlett was used to dictating the rules. They had to be able to work together.

'I'm not planning on being here very long,' she said. Firm and decisive.

'Ouch.' But he didn't seem to be offended. He was smiling, obviously not taking her seriously despite her outfit and her no-nonsense tone. 'What about something to eat?' he asked. 'Have you had dinner?'

'I'm fine.'

She waited as he ordered their drinks and a serve of beef sliders with fries. He handed her a glass of wine and led her to a table in the corner. It was hot in the pub and Scarlett could feel herself starting to perspire. The back of her neck was damp under her bun. The heat was making breathing difficult, or maybe it was Jake's proximity—he had chosen the chair at right angles to hers, not opposite, and his knee brushed against hers as he sat. She slipped her jacket off, deciding that if he wasn't going to heed her power-dressing message she may as well be comfortable, but she sat, upright, tense and stiff on her chair.

'You can relax,' he told her. 'I can be trusted to keep my hands to myself, much as I would like to do otherwise.' His gaze ran down the length of her arm, from her bare shoulder to her wrist, and Scarlett imagined she could feel a trail of heat on her skin. She shifted in her chair, hoping that another inch of space would break the sensation.

Jake was still smiling. He sipped his beer and said, 'I apologise if my being at the hospital makes you uncomfortable but the fact of the matter is I'm there for the next four weeks so we're going to come into contact with each other. Why is that a problem for you?'

'It's not, as long as we agree to forget about Saturday night. I don't want anyone to know about that.'

'I don't think I can forget about it but I guess I can refrain from mentioning it, but only if you give me a good reason.'

'There're a dozen reasons why. You're a med student. I'm a registrar. I've worked really hard to get to where I am and I don't want to give people a reason to take it away from me.'

'What reason could this give them?'

But Scarlett didn't answer that question as something else occurred to her. 'Is that why you slept with me? Because we were going to be working together? Were you hoping it was going to work in your favour somehow?'

'You asked me in. Remember? Actually, dragged me in might be a better description.' He grinned.

She couldn't remember exactly how he'd ended up inside her house but she did know she hadn't wanted him to leave. But her final choice may have been different if she'd known what the future held. 'I never would have slept with you if I'd known you were going to turn up at my work.'

'So I just have to wait until my placement is finished and then you'll date me.'

'I don't want to date you,' she said.

'I think you do.'

He was smiling again and his smile went deep to her core, stoking the fire that smouldered in her belly just waiting for his touch. She should have ordered a soft drink, not wine, she thought as her resolve weakened with every glance.

'No, I don't,' she said, trying to find that firm, decisive tone she desperately needed. 'I want to pretend that Saturday night never happened and hope that people don't find out. I've worked hard to get where I am. I have a plan and I don't want to jeopardise it by having people look at me differently. I don't have any intention of telling anyone about Saturday night. One-night stands are not my thing.'

Jake took a draught of his beer. She could see him trying to hide a smile.

'Why are you still smiling?'

'Because if one-night hook-ups are out of character for you then maybe I'm in with a chance of getting you to make it two.'

'You could have any woman you wanted. Why me?'

'You have that super-sexy secretary thing going on.'

'You think I look like a secretary?'

'Maybe not so much a secretary, maybe more a high-school principal,' he said. 'When you're dressed all neat and businesslike in your suit and your tidy hair and sitting there bossing me around, I feel like I'm back in the principal's office.'

The picture he painted made her laugh. She'd suspected he had a bit of a rebellious streak. 'Good. That should stop you from wanting to ask me out.'

Jake grinned. 'I dunno, she was pretty hot. And now that I know what happens when you strip back the layers and let your hair down...' He raised an eyebrow and shrugged. 'I had a really good time on Saturday night and, yes, I'd like to do it again,' he said simply, as the waitress placed his meal on the table. 'If I'm prepared to wait until I finish my placement, tell me why I shouldn't ask you out on a proper date.'

'You really want to take me out on a date?'

He nodded.

'But I'm not your type.'

'What is my type?'

'Someone more your own age.'

'How old do you think I am?'

She let her eyes travel over his face. Along the sharp edges of his jaw, across the smooth skin of his cheekbones, blemish- and wrinkle-free, the only lines on his face were smile lines. Her eyes met his. He was watching her just as intently. She reached across the table and pinched a few chips from his plate just to break eye contact as she answered, 'Twenty-three.'

'I'm twenty-six,' he said. 'I had a circuitous path to med school,' he explained, 'but that must put us close enough in age. So now will you date me?'

Scarlett shook her head. 'No. I'm still not your type.'

'And what makes you think you know what my type is?'

'I imagine it would be someone who is used to going clubbing, partying until the early morning.'

'That sounds like you.'

'If I'm out at two in the morning it's because I've been at work. Going clubbing is not my thing.'

'What is your thing?'

The rest of the bar receded into the distance as Jake

looked at her. He leant towards her and Scarlett could feel herself being drawn in. He really was far too cute and she was struggling to remember what her thing was. She could feel herself growing warm under his gaze, her skin was burning but she'd already taken her jacket off and she had no more clothing to shed.

'I'm not sure but it's not going home with men who I meet in strip clubs.'

'I beg to differ.'

'I'm not going to date you.' She shook her head again, trying to convince herself as much as him that she meant every word.

'We'll see,' he said.

'You're not listening to me,' she replied, as she reached for her glass of wine. Jake reached for the salt at the same time and his hand brushed her forearm. Scarlett froze, immobilised by the current that raced up her arm. Her gaze dropped to his hand as he lightly curled his fingers around her arm and ran them along the sensitive skin to her wrist. She held her breath, waiting for him to stop touching her but hoping he wouldn't. She was a mess of contradictions. Her body wanted him; it felt as though every cell was straining towards him and clearly ignoring what her mind dictated and Scarlett wasn't sure whether her mind was strong enough to counteract the physical pull.

Jake was watching her watching him, as his fingers came to rest on her skin. 'I am listening,' he said. 'I hear what you're saying and I know you were intent on putting me straight tonight. I've heard what you've said and I see what you're wearing. Don't think I haven't noticed you've ditched your stripper heels in favour of something more demure, but I can also see your reaction to me and your body language is telling me something completely different.'

'That's just chemistry. A physical reaction.'

'And it should be celebrated. We both enjoyed Saturday night—why deny yourself pleasure?'

'But that's my point. Everything about Saturday night was completely out of character for me.'

'You don't like having a good time?'

'I'm not denying I had fun but it was only ever meant to be one night. I didn't think I'd ever see you again.'

'But that's what I don't understand. Why can't we do this again?'

'Because I have a plan.' Scarlett took a deep breath. She had one chance to convince him that getting involved would be a mistake. She had to convince him because by doing so she hoped she would convince herself. She moved her arm, removing herself from his touch as she sorted through her words. 'Usually I make carefully considered decisions. Usually I think about the consequences. Saturday night was just a lapse of control and I'm putting it down to a stressful week and one too many cocktails.'

'It was consensual, wasn't it? You told me you knew what you were doing.'

Scarlett nodded. 'I knew exactly what I was doing,' she admitted, 'but my point is I only intended to do it once.'

'That's a pity. Life should be fun.'

But in Scarlett's opinion life was meant to be taken seriously. That was the way to keep control. She wasn't young and irresponsible like Rose, she had never been like that, and she wasn't carefree and spontaneous like Ruby.

She stood and collected her jacket. She took a ten-dollar note from her purse and left it on the table to pay for her drink. She didn't want to be indebted to Jake.

'I'm sorry,' she told him. 'I have a plan and you don't fit into it.'

Firm and decisive.

And miserable.

But it was for the best.

CHAPTER FOUR

JAKE HAD EVERY intention of respecting Scarlett's wishes. As much as he didn't like, or even agree with, her decision he wasn't going to make her life difficult by making a nuisance of himself. If she didn't want to have anything to do with him he had to respect that. He had been raised to respect women and that included respecting their decisions.

He didn't need to be dating. His final year of studies and his part-time job at The Coop kept him busy enough. University life was almost over and he had to make sure he graduated well if he wanted to be accepted into the hospital of his choice for his intern year. Scarlett was right—scandal was best avoided. He didn't want to jeopardise his career chances any more than she did.

He decided he would respect her conditions for now and he wouldn't ask her out again while they were working together, but once his placement was finished he would see how things lay between them then. Their chemistry had been too good to just let her go without a little bit of a fight.

It would be easy to find things to occupy his time for the remainder of the placement, especially if the last few days were anything to go by. Their paths had barely crossed so his resolve wasn't tested.

Three more weeks, he told himself. He could wait that long, he thought as he glanced at the file in his hand. A twenty-nine-year-old female had presented to Emergency with abdominal pain. He pulled back the curtain and ducked inside the treatment cubicle. The busier he was the faster time would pass.

The woman lay on the bed, curled on her side, with her anxious-looking partner sitting beside her. He stood as soon as Jake drew the curtain behind him but his movement was restricted by his partner, who kept a tense grip on his hand.

'Doctor, you have to do something, my wife is in terrible pain.' He didn't wait for Jake to introduce himself.

'Is it the baby?' the woman asked. She was the same age as Scarlett and she also had thick, dark hair, but the similarities ended there. Her face was pinched with pain and the knuckles on her right hand were white as she squeezed her partner's fingers.

'You're pregnant?' Jake hadn't noticed that on the file but he hadn't had much chance to look at it.

The woman nodded.

'How many weeks?' She was several kilograms overweight so it was difficult to judge.

'Six.' So her extra weight wasn't all pregnancy-related and there was a chance that she may have been mistaken with dates, one way or the other.

'Have you had the pregnancy confirmed?'

'We did a home test yesterday. It was positive,' the husband replied.

A positive home pregnancy test at this early stage was an indicator but not, in Jake's opinion, full confirmation. He knew he had to treat that news as an unconfirmed pregnancy until he had a chance to do more tests. But an ectopic pregnancy could be the cause of her symptoms and he would need to keep that in mind, although he couldn't afford to rule out appendicitis or other abdominal disorders. He couldn't be influenced by the couple's suppositions. He needed to confirm a diagnosis, not play guessing games, and to do that he needed more information.

'I'm a final-year medical student—'

'My wife is pregnant and she's bleeding,' the husband interrupted Jake. 'We want to see a *doctor*.'

'The doctors are all busy,' Jake said, concentrating hard to keep his tone even. He addressed his next sentence to the wife. 'You're welcome to wait until one is available but I can't tell you how long that will be.' He suspected she wouldn't want to wait. 'I need to get some details and then I'll call a doctor when we know what is happening,' he explained. 'I can get started with your medical history and the physical exam and a doctor will join us when one becomes available.'

The look of nervousness he had seen earlier in the wife's eyes disappeared. She was in pain and he knew she wouldn't want to wait. A final-year medical student was close enough to the real thing for her. 'Okay,' she replied. Jake could almost see the husband deflate as his wife's agreement took the puff out of him.

Jake called for a nurse. He recorded the details of Angela's symptoms, their onset and severity, her menstrual history and her activities over the past twenty-four hours. He got the nurse to collect a urine sample so he could run a pregnancy test and then he began the physical exam. The medical history he'd taken made him suspect that an ectopic pregnancy was likely to be the cause of her pain but he wanted more confirmation.

'We need a pelvic ultrasound,' he told the nurse.

Sally ducked out of the cubicle to organise the equipment but she couldn't have been more than a few steps away when Angela cried out. She clutched her stomach and bent her knees to her chest. Jake looked at her in alarm. Her face was completely white and beads of perspiration had broken out across her forehead and upper lip.

A ruptured fallopian tube or burst appendix raced to the top of the list of possible diagnoses. The quickest way to find out the answer now was to open her up.

'Sally!' he called out. The nurse stuck her head back in and Jake tried to disguise the note of panic he suspected was evident in his voice as he told her, 'I need a gynae consult. Right now.'

Scarlett checked over her equipment, ready to anaesthetise her patient as soon as Diana, the gynaecologist, was ready. Their patient, a twenty-nine-year-old woman, was about to undergo surgery for a ruptured Fallopian tube. Apparently she had presented to Emergency with abdominal pain from an ectopic pregnancy and things had gone downhill from there. The general consensus was she was lucky that she'd already been in the hospital and therefore only minutes from help.

She turned her head as she heard the sucking sound of the theatre door as it was opened. Her heart tumbled in her chest as she saw Diana walk in, followed by Jake. He was looking straight at her, his green eyes clear and confident. He was tying his mask and the bottom half of his face was obscured but she didn't need to see all of his features. She'd recognise his green eyes anywhere; the corners crinkled as he smiled at her. She nodded a greeting in return. Her face seemed to have frozen— surprise had taken away her ability to smile.

His mask was green and matched his eyes perfectly.

She wondered if he had chosen it deliberately but then she doubted he would have thought of that. While he was gorgeous looking with a body to match she couldn't accuse him of being vain.

He had short-sleeved scrubs on and Scarlett could see the bottom three stars of the tattoo on the inside of his left triceps. It gave her a little thrill to know the reason behind the tattoo. Having that knowledge seemed like such a personal thing and he had shared it with her on the night they had made love. He'd had the Southern Cross constellation tattooed on his arm before he'd taken off overseas for a gap year after finishing school to remind him of where he came from and to remind him that he always planned to come home.

They had lain together in her bed after making love. Jake had wrapped his right arm around her shoulders as she'd lain with her head on his chest and let her fingers trail over the ridges of his stomach muscles. His left hand had been tucked behind his head, in much the same position as it was now, and Scarlett had lifted her hand from his abdominals to run her fingers over each little star. She'd expected the stars to feel bumpy and raised but they had been smooth and flat on his skin. Just the memory of it now made her heartbeat quicken.

He tied the mask easily. He looked perfectly at home in Theatre. He didn't look like a student. He looked comfortable, he looked like he belonged. But Scarlett suspected he wasn't the type of person who would feel uncomfortable anywhere. He'd certainly seemed at home half-naked on a stage in front of a crowd of women so she supposed this setting would be a piece of cake. Two female doctors, two female nurses and Jake—it would be nothing out of the ordinary for him.

Scarlett finally recovered control of her facial muscles and was able to murmur a greeting as Diana introduced Jake and explained that he had been doing the consult when Angela's fallopian tube had ruptured and Diana had invited him to observe Theatre.

'If you stand just to my left you should get a good view of the surgery,' Diana told him.

Scarlett focussed on putting Angela to sleep as she tried to block out the picture of Diana and Jake standing shoulder to shoulder and tried to ignore the tightening of her stomach that she recognised as jealousy. She knew she was being ridiculous. They were only standing together and she had no right to be jealous but Diana was making her a bit crazy. Diana had a reputation as a serial dater around the hospital and Scarlett could imagine her wanting a taste of Jake, but surely not even Diana would sleep with a student?

Diana had made an incision into Angela's abdomen and confirmed what Jake had suspected. Angela had an ectopic pregnancy that had ruptured her fallopian tube.

'This was her first pregnancy, is that right?' she asked Jake.

'Yes. She and her husband said they'd been trying for a while.'

'I think I can repair the tube. I'm going to try,' she said, and explained her reasoning. 'Having one ectopic pregnancy increases her chances of having subsequent ectopic pregnancies. She won't thank me if I don't try to save the tube if it's at all possible. I can't afford to be careless with another woman's fertility.'

Scarlett couldn't fault Diana's skills as a doctor or surgeon but she couldn't help feeling her blood boil as she watched the surgery. As she watched Diana's arm brush against Jake's as she repaired and stitched. But Scarlett knew this was her issue, not Diana's.

Jake was paying close attention to the surgery, asking questions as he looked over Diana's shoulder. Scarlett imagined that Diana could feel Jake's breath on her cheek, just like she had on Saturday night, and she knew she wanted to be the one whose arm was brushing against his.

He hadn't spoken to her. He hadn't looked at her and Scarlett suspected that maybe he was deliberately avoiding her. She didn't want to be ignored. She wasn't sure what she wanted but it wasn't that. Not wanting to show that she was bothered by the lack of attention, she pretended to adjust her equipment but in reality everything was going smoothly with the sedation and there was no need for her to do anything other than monitor the machine.

'Right, that's looking good. I'm really pleased with that outcome.' Diana had managed to repair the tube and was sewing up the incision. There was a noticeable decrease in the tension in Theatre as Diana announced success.

'Scarlett, now the crisis is over there's something I wanted to speak to you about,' Diana said as she snipped a thread. 'I was thinking of asking Richard if he wanted to come with me to Candice's wedding but I wanted to make sure I wasn't stepping on your toes. It is over between the two of you, isn't it?'

Scarlett was mortified. She could feel her cheeks flushing and she was glad her face was half-hidden behind a mask. She would love to have some of Diana's confidence, even ten per cent would be good. She could never imagine announcing her dating plans to a room full of colleagues. But that wasn't the only difference between the two of them.

She had to answer Diana. She couldn't pretend she

hadn't spoken directly to her. She looked up and her gaze landed on Jake first. He was watching her from behind Diana's shoulder.

Now he watched her!

Immediately she could feel heat flooding through her. She hated having such primeval reactions to him when he seemed quite unflustered but it reinforced her feeling that she had made the right decision by staying away from him. Nothing good could come from any involvement. She knew there was a good chance she would lose control.

She quickly averted her gaze, looking at Diana instead. She was a few years older than Scarlett, somewhere in her early thirties. Scarlett wondered if she knew Richard's biological clock was ticking but it wasn't up to her to tell her. Diana might well be hearing the same ticking as Richard. It wasn't Scarlett's business anymore.

'As far as I'm concerned, Richard is a free agent,' she told Diana. 'But I know he's already accepted an invitation to Candice's wedding and I'm pretty sure he'll still be planning to attend. Were you going to ask him as your date?'

'Not yet. I know he's already going but I thought it was a good opportunity to go together without any pressure.'

Scarlett thought inviting someone to a wedding as a first date, even an unofficial one, was buried in pressure. It was a gutsy move but she was actually relieved that Diana had set her sights on Richard as it meant Jake was safe. If Scarlett couldn't have him she didn't want anyone else to either.

'I'm sure he'd be flattered by your attention,' Scarlett said. She could feel Jake watching her still but she avoided his gaze by keeping her eyes glued to her monitors until it was time to reverse the anaesthetic.

But Jake followed her out of Theatre.

'Diana was talking about Richard Thomas, the plastic surgeon, wasn't she?' he asked, as they stripped off their masks and caps.

Scarlett looked down at her hands as she peeled off her gloves. She didn't need to see what she was doing but it allowed her to avoid eye contact. She threw her gloves in the bin as she replied, 'Yes.'

'You could date Richard but not me?' Jake kept the volume of his words low but Scarlett could hear the irritation in his voice. 'Don't you think that's a bit hypocritical?'

'Richard is a senior consultant, no one thinks there's anything wrong with a registrar dating a senior.'

'You don't think people might think you're sleeping your way to the top?'

Scarlett was about to deny his ridiculous accusation but then hesitated. Would people have thought that? Maybe. Not that she would admit he might be right.

Although she had to admit that she'd known dating Richard wouldn't hurt her career prospects so perhaps she was guilty as charged.

She could feel her temper rising. Jake could certainly push her buttons and it annoyed her that he could make her second-guess herself. But she knew it was more than that. All her reactions to him were extreme and she hated losing control but that seemed to be a permanent hazard when she was around him. Extreme irritation. Extreme arousal. Extreme attraction. Extreme awareness. Every reaction, every one of her senses, became heightened in response to him.

'If a registrar can date a senior, why can't a registrar date an intern?' he asked.

'I'm sure they do but you're not an intern. You're still a student.'

'I won't always be. When I'm a registrar and you're a consultant, what will your excuse be then? Is this about me or you?'

She was normally calm, collected and controlled but she seemed to have trouble keeping a lid on her emotions around Jake. She shouldn't be having this conversation with him. She should just walk away but she couldn't make her feet move. She was attracted to him, she wasn't denying that, but once again it was her issue. She had a plan, she was determined to qualify as an anaesthesiologist and she wasn't going to be distracted by an emotion as basic as lust. Not when it could cost her her career.

'This is about both of us. I'm sure we'd be violating all sorts of workplace policies by dating and I for one don't want to be accused of sexual harassment. I am not prepared to jeopardise my career. No matter how tempted I am, nothing is worth that.'

'How about if we keep it low key? Take a leaf out of Diana's book and go to Candice's wedding together. As colleagues. Nothing more.'

'Richard hasn't accepted Diana's invitation yet,' Scarlett was quick to point out.

'Fair enough, but there's no reason to think he won't. She's a good-looking woman, smart, single, he's got no reason not to accept.'

Scarlett felt her stomach clench with another burst of jealousy. Not over the idea of Richard and Diana but because Jake had called her good looking.

'I don't need a lift, thank you, I'm going with my

sister Ruby. She used to work with Candice and she's coming to town for the wedding.'

'Is she the one who owns the sexy shoes?'

He was smiling at her, his cheeky grin lighting up his eyes, seemingly unbothered by her rejection of his offer. Did nothing faze him? Was he always so relaxed and easygoing?

She shook her head. 'No, those were Rose's.'

'Another sister? How many do you have?'

'Only two.'

Talking about Ruby made her realise she would provide the perfect distraction. She decided she would focus on Ruby's visit. Ruby always blew into town like a mini-tornado and her sister's presence should be enough to keep her occupied *and* keep her mind off Jake. Ruby would give her enough to worry about and leave no time for sexy med students. Ruby was the perfect solution to her dilemma.

CHAPTER FIVE

SCARLETT SCANNED THE crowd as the passengers disembarked from the plane and were disgorged up the ramp and into the terminal. She hadn't seen Ruby for several months and although they kept in regular contact with phone calls and social media it wasn't the same as seeing each other in person. Scarlett paced impatiently. She was dying to give Ruby a big hug and to immerse herself in her sister's latest news. She always had a story to tell.

Ruby was the middle of the three Anderson sisters. Rose was the baby of the family and Scarlett the sensible, oldest sister. Ruby was the wild child, the sister who tried whatever she liked and did whatever she pleased. Scarlett used to wish she was that brave but the fact of the matter was she wasn't brave or rebellious or foolhardy. She was cautious, pragmatic and reliable, and she'd had to decide long ago to let Ruby have the adventures. And Ruby did. There was no denying that Ruby lived her life fully and Scarlett always enjoyed spending time with her, even though it could be exhausting. Ruby was more than a breath of fresh air in Scarlett's world, she was a whirlwind.

The two of them hadn't always been close and there had been plenty of differences of opinion as they'd been growing up. Ruby had caused their mother plenty of headaches and to compensate for Ruby's headstrong behaviour Scarlett had always tried to do the right thing to avoid causing any further stress. She knew that sometimes she'd resented Ruby and her carefree and occasionally selfish attitude but as she'd matured, as they'd both matured, their differences had diminished. When Ruby had left home ten years ago, at the age of sixteen, Scarlett had missed her terribly. And although Ruby had come and gone, she'd never officially returned to South Australia and now Scarlett made sure to make the most of their time together.

A tall, thin woman with shoulder-length platinum-blond curls was walking briskly along the edge of the ramp, dodging fellow passengers and waving. It took Scarlett a moment to realise it was Ruby. Last time she had been home her natural strawberry blond locks had been dyed a dark red but the platinum shade was just as striking and probably better suited to her fair colouring.

Scarlett waved back and took in Ruby's outfit as she waited for her to reach the end of the ramp. Ruby's fashion choices were always interesting and today was no exception. The majority of Ruby's clothes came from markets and second-hand stores and Byron Bay, her current home town, had no shortage of either. Scarlett was constantly amazed that she chose to buy her clothes this way. After wearing second-hand clothes for most of their childhood, Scarlett had vowed she would always have new clothes and the more expensive the better. She chose to save her money and buy a few classic pieces each season, but not Ruby. Ruby was migratory and whenever she moved she'd leave most of her wardrobe behind, donated back to the second-hand clothes stores where it had come from, and pick

up thrift-shop clothes that blended into her new envi-
ronment when she relocated.

Today she was wearing a floaty, ankle-length, tie-
dyed skirt with a tight black T-shirt emblazoned with
what looked like a movie poster but it wasn't a movie
Scarlett recognised. She looked like a stereotypical
Byron Bay hippie. A multitude of different-coloured
bangles adorned her wrists and ankles and her toenails
were painted a bright tangerine. In contrast to her toenails, her fingernails were short, clean and unpainted—
nurse's fingernails.

Despite her mismatched outfit she looked clean and
fresh. Her hair was newly washed, her face make-up
free. Her pale, flawless skin didn't need any help other
than a lick of mascara for her eyelashes. Ruby looked
like her father's side of the family. There were physical
similarities to Rose, particularly now that Ruby's hair
was blond, but Scarlett knew that she and Ruby looked
nothing alike. And it wasn't just their taste in clothes.

Scarlett hugged her the minute she stepped off the
ramp. She was skin and bone.

'You're so thin.'

'I've been too busy to eat.' Ruby grinned as Scarlett released her.

Scarlett recognised that look. 'You know you can
stop having sex to eat,' she teased. 'Who is he?'

'Who *was* he, you mean.'

Ruby's relationships never lasted very long and it
was almost always Ruby who did the leaving.

'Okay. I'll bite. Who was he?' Scarlett amended as
she led the way to her car.

'He was a movie director.'

'You haven't taken up acting now, have you?'

While Ruby chopped and changed hairstyles, ad-

dresses and boyfriends almost as often as she changed
her underwear, the one thing that had been constant in
her life had been her job. Ruby was a nurse, and had
nursed with Candice in Melbourne, hence the invitation to the wedding, and it was something that Scarlett
thought she loved. While many other things about Ruby
wouldn't surprise her, finding out she'd quit nursing
would be unexpected.

'No, no.' Ruby laughed. 'He was directing a small-
budget indie flick that was being filmed on the Central
Coast, in and around Byron Bay.'

'How on earth did you meet him?' Scarlett asked, as
Ruby threw her duffel bag into the car. Scarlett eyed the
bag suspiciously. She couldn't imagine what Ruby had
packed in there to wear to Candice's wedding. Whatever it was would surely be creased beyond recognition.

'There was an accident on set. Rohan brought the
injured actor into the hospital.'

Scarlett was amazed at the different types of men
Ruby had dated. In recent memory there had been a
pharmacist, a guy who ran a surf school, a teacher and
now a movie director, which probably explained Ruby's
T-shirt, but Scarlett couldn't work out what they could
possibly have in common.

'So what attracted you to him?' Scarlett asked, as she
started the car and drove out of the car park.

'He was interesting. They all are. I like a guy who
can give me new experiences. Not just in the bedroom,'
she said in response to Scarlett's silent smirk, 'although
I'm not opposed to that either, but I like seeing the
world through different eyes. I guess, most importantly,
there's always a connection, some chemistry. And that's
hard to resist. When that happens I know I just have to

give him a try. If they're good in bed, I'll keep them around for a bit. If they're not...*sayonara*.'

Scarlett thought she understood that feeling now. It was how she felt about Jake and that just served to confirm her idea that he was okay for a fling. Ruby's relationships never lasted long. Obviously chemistry was enough to sustain a short-term fling but did something that burned so brightly fizzle out just as rapidly? It certainly seemed to be the case for Ruby. Jake was sexy and fun but a very unlikely match for herself. She knew someone like Richard, someone meticulous and serious, would be a far better fit for her. If Jake was going to be anything to her it could only be temporary.

'What happened to this one?'

Ruby shrugged. 'They finished filming.'

'Did he break your heart?'

Ruby laughed. 'No. It was fun while it lasted but if he hadn't had to pack up and move on I would have moved on anyway. I was getting bored.'

'At least it means you have time to eat again,' Scarlett told her as she parked the car in front of her house. 'Which is good because we're having lunch with Mum.'

'Really?'

Scarlett could hear the note of trepidation in Ruby's voice. Ruby had a volatile relationship with their mother, which had become strained when Ruby had been a teenager and they had never recovered an easy camaraderie. Scarlett knew Ruby felt as though her mother was constantly disappointed in her. She felt their mother judged her sister and found her lacking. And despite the fact that Ruby had straightened out her life, more or less, she never believed Scarlett when she tried to tell her that their mother loved her and just wanted to feel included in Ruby's life.

Ruby's unpredictable relationship with their mother was one reason she usually crashed at Scarlett's place when she visited. It was always better if Ruby and Lucy had their own space.

'We'll just have a quick lunch and then we'll come back here to get ready for the wedding. Have you got something to wear in there?' Scarlett asked, as Ruby dumped her duffel bag in the spare bedroom.

'Of course. I might even have something to lend to you.'

Scarlett raised her eyebrows. She couldn't imagine that she'd be able to fit into anything of Ruby's. While they were a similar height, Ruby's stick-thin figure was quite the opposite of Scarlett's curves.

'What time is Richard picking us up for the wedding?' Ruby wanted to know.

'He's not. Mel is going to swing past in a cab for us just before four.'

Ruby was frowning. 'Is Richard working?'

'No. We're not together anymore.'

'You're kidding.' Ruby plopped herself on the bed. 'What happened?'

Scarlett hadn't intended to tell Ruby about breaking up with Richard right at this minute, she'd planned to ease into that conversation, but there was no way to avoid the question now.

'Is he still planning on going to the wedding?' Ruby asked when Scarlett had finished giving her the abbreviated version of events. 'Is it going to be awkward?'

'It'll be fine.' Scarlett didn't bother to explain that Richard had accepted Diana's invitation and would be accompanying her to the wedding. That wouldn't matter to Ruby.

'I asked Candice to put me with some hot single guys,' Ruby announced. 'Maybe she's put us together.'

Scarlett immediately wondered if Candice might have put her on the same table as Jake. It had been at least twenty minutes since she'd last thought of him— that had to be counted as progress.

'We can find ourselves a couple of eligible bachelors and organise a double date.' Ruby immediately started thinking about picking up guys at the wedding, which was why Scarlett hadn't intended to say anything about Richard. She'd had some disastrous dating experiences with Ruby in the past. Their taste in men was about as different as their taste in clothes. Conservative and sensible was Scarlett's motto, which was why Jake was so not her type, and she didn't think she'd ever heard Ruby even *use* the word 'conservative', except maybe to describe Scarlett,

'Or do you already have another beau waiting in the wings?' Ruby asked, when Scarlett didn't reply.

She shook her head. 'I'm not like you. I can't just go from one man to the next.' She wished she could. She wished she didn't have her goals set. She wished she could just be with Jake, even temporarily, without worrying about the consequences. Even though she'd been the one to lay down the rules she had struggled to put him out of her thoughts. He had kept his part of the bargain and had kept his distance around the hospital, but she had been aware of him watching her and she could always tell the exact moment he was anywhere in her vicinity. Her body seemed attuned to his presence; it seemed to pick up his frequency before her brain had registered it. The more she told herself to ignore him the more often she noticed him.

She kept up a constant stream of questions to Ruby as

she drove to their mother's house, hoping that listening to Ruby chatter would keep thoughts of Jake at bay. It worked, sort of. And whatever part of her brain wasn't taken up with Ruby's conversation was soon occupied with concern for their mother, who seemed to age noticeably every time Scarlett saw her.

Lucy was only forty-seven but could have been mistaken for someone five, if not ten years older. She was an older, more tired version of Scarlett. They had the same thick chestnut hair but while Scarlett's was still dark, her mother's was streaked with grey. They shared the same dark eyes but Lucy's were underscored with deep shadows and Scarlett knew that her mother's figure had once looked like hers but three pregnancies and years of shiftwork and irregular meals as a nurse had combined to sap Lucy's vitality.

This was what Scarlett feared her own future would look like if she succumbed and travelled down the marriage and babies path. In her opinion and experience there wasn't much to recommend it.

The conversation started with the usual discussion about their various careers but Scarlett knew she was on tenterhooks, waiting for something to be said that would set the cat among the pigeons.

It wasn't long before Lucy changed the topic. 'So you haven't settled down yet, Ruby?'

Scarlett held her breath as she wished, not for the first time, that Ruby drank alcohol. She was sure a glass of wine would help to mellow the different personalities and ease the tension but she knew Ruby had perfectly valid reasons for her abstinence and Scarlett couldn't argue with those. She waited for Ruby's response.

'Mum, I'm twenty-six, settling down is the last thing on my mind. I'm in the prime of my life and I intend to have fun while I can. Scarlett is the one you need to talk to. Do you know she's broken up with Richard?'

Scarlett had expected to hear Ruby's usual announcement that she was far too young to even think about settling down but she hadn't expected her to deflect attention from herself by announcing Scarlett's own news.

'Scarlett? When did that happen? Why didn't you tell me?'

Ruby's tactic seemed to have worked. Lucy forgot her usual retort, which went along the lines of the fact that she'd had three children by the time she was twenty-six, which then inevitably led to the argument that only one of those pregnancies had actually been planned and Ruby didn't intend to follow that path. Ruby had a point but although Lucy may not have been terribly successful in either her family planning or in choosing the fathers of her children, she had done her best to raise her daughters. Scarlett knew it had never been Lucy's intention to have three children by three different men but it was the way things had worked out.

Lucy had been a single parent for most of Scarlett's twenty-nine years. She had given birth to Scarlett just after her eighteenth birthday and Scarlett had always felt an obligation to protect her mother as much as possible. Lucy had been unlucky in love and Scarlett also knew that Ruby and Rose, to a lesser degree, had tested Lucy's patience and therefore Scarlett had tried not to add to her mother's burden. She hadn't told her mother about the break-up because she didn't want Lucy worrying about her.

'Are you okay?' Lucy asked, when Scarlett wasn't quick enough with an explanation.

'I'm fine. It was my decision.'

'But why? What went wrong? I thought Richard was what you wanted.'

Richard might have been what she wanted but it had turned out he hadn't been *who* she wanted. If she'd had a checklist she would have put plenty of ticks beside his name, beginning with the fact that he was older than her, settled in his career and didn't want children. She didn't really have an aversion to having a family but she was terrified of being left to raise them alone, like her mother had been. If she was ever going to have kids she'd make damn sure it was with someone who loved her. And there was no guarantee that even that would be enough. Therefore it was safer not to reproduce. In her mind it was safer not to put herself in that situation, although if Richard hadn't changed his mind she may well have stayed with him. She'd even thought she loved him.

Until she'd met Jake.

Whether or not it was simply a matter of timing or circumstances, she hadn't been able to resist Jake. Which meant she couldn't have been in love with Richard, could she? Not when she'd been so quick to fall for Jake's charms and jump into his bed. Ruby bed-hopped but to her credit she had never professed or even pretended to be in love. Scarlett knew now that she had been pretending with Richard.

'I didn't love him.' That was the simplest explanation and the one that would lead to the least amount of questioning.

Scarlett knew her mother had been not so secretly hoping she would marry Richard. Or someone like him. Someone who could take care of her financially and give her the security she had never had. Scarlett had to admit that security was something she craved too but she intended to rely on herself, not another person, for that security. If she was going to get married it would be because she needed something only that other person could give her. It wouldn't be for something she could provide for herself. Her mother had lost one partner to illness, one had simply left and the other had been booted out. Through her mother's misfortunes Scarlett had learnt not to rely on anyone but herself.

Scarlett looked at Lucy. She was so afraid of ending up like her, old and alone. But as much as she didn't want to be alone, she was more afraid of being left. And Richard's heart attack had given her a glimpse of the future and that terrified her.

Somehow both she and Ruby managed to get through lunch relatively unscathed but Scarlett was relieved to get home and focus on getting ready for Candice's wedding.

She got out of the shower and stuck her head into the spare bedroom to see what Ruby was wearing. Ruby had dried her hair and had swept it to one side before tucking the end up so it curled and sat just below her jawline. But that was all she'd done. She was still wrapped in her towel.

'Not dressed yet?' Scarlett asked.

In answer, Ruby pulled a slim parcel, wrapped in tissue paper, from her duffel bag. She unwrapped it to reveal a royal blue silk tank-top, heavily embroidered from the shoulders to the waist. Embroidery was another fashion trend that was loved in Byron Bay but at least this garment actually looked new and wasn't tie-dyed, Scarlett thought as Ruby dropped her towel, pulled on some knickers and shimmied into the top.

She didn't bother with a bra; she didn't need one. The

top hung loosely from her shoulders and fell just a few inches below her butt. Scarlett waited to see what pants Ruby was going to wear but she just slipped her feet into a pair of strappy silver heels and appeared to be done.

Scarlett raised her eyebrows. 'Is that what you're wearing?'

'What's wrong?' Ruby looked down at her feet. She pulled out another pair of shoes. Neutral peeptoe wedges with an ankle strap. 'These are the only other shoes I have. I think the silver ones go best with the dress.'

So it *was* a dress. 'I wasn't talking about the shoes.'

'What's the matter, then? Don't I look all right?'

Actually, she looked amazing. The 'dress' skimmed perfectly over her long, lean figure and she could get away with the short length as she had fantastic legs. Good legs, courtesy of their mother, were probably the one thing she and Ruby and Rose did have in common, that and the same shoe size. Scarlett couldn't fault Ruby for having the confidence to wear the outfit. Not when she looked so gorgeous. 'You look fabulous.'

'Thanks,' Ruby said, as she twirled in front of the mirror. She was a girl who was used to receiving compliments and she wasn't really looking for approval. 'Now it's your turn. What are you wearing?'

Ruby followed Scarlett into her room and waited as Scarlett pulled her dress from the wardrobe. It was a simple sleeveless shift dress, knee-length and panelled. The centre panel had a floral pattern and the sides were black and cut in at the waist to take the emphasis away from the hips and draw the eye in.

'You can't wear that,' Ruby said.

'Why not?'

'It's okay for an office party or a lunch but it's too

casual for an evening wedding and it'll make you look old. I'll find you something else.' Ruby pulled no punches as she began to rummage through the wardrobe. Scarlett had thought the floral fabric gave the dress a fun, celebratory air but Ruby obviously thought otherwise.

'What about this?' Ruby was holding up a silk shirt dress that Scarlett had bought to wear as a top. It had a boat neck, a gathered waist and loose, elbow-length sleeves. In keeping with the sixties style, the fabric was printed with a paisley pattern in pale pink, cream and green.

'I don't know. I haven't got the right pants to wear with it.' Scarlett had intended to wear it with skinny satin pants but all she had were black ones and they had looked wrong against the colour and pattern of the top and she hadn't managed to find the right alternative colour yet.

'Pants! Who said anything about pants?' Ruby cried. 'This is a dress. Put it on, let's have a look.'

Scarlett found her underwear, there was no chance of going braless with DD breasts, and then pulled the dress over her head. It fell to mid-thigh and was much shorter than anything she would normally wear but still several inches longer than the dress Ruby had on.

Ruby was searching the bottom of the wardrobe for shoes. Scarlett would have to remind her not to bend over at the wedding unless she wanted to give all the other guests a glimpse of her undies. She pulled out a pair of neutral pumps and held them out in front of her, her head turned to one side as she looked at them with the dress. She screwed up her nose. The shoes were obviously not to her liking.

'Do you have anything else in this colour?'

Scarlett shook her head.

'That's okay, I'll lend you mine.'

Scarlett smiled to herself; Jake was going to think she didn't own any shoes of her own. *Stop it. Stop thinking about him.*

Ruby disappeared to her room and came back with her nude wedges. 'These will be better.'

Scarlett slipped them on. They were a good choice, the right colour and a better fit stylewise, plus they made her legs look exceptionally long. The floaty sleeves and the neckline preserved enough of her modesty to ensure that overall the outfit wasn't too revealing. It was a win-win.

'Perfect,' Ruby declared. 'Now for hair and make-up. Sit on the bed and I'll fix you up.'

Ruby might not believe in make-up for herself but she had a natural flair for colour and for the dramatic and by the time she'd finished Scarlett felt pretty enough, even if she didn't quite look like herself. But that was okay, she could think of her make-up as war paint. Ruby's ministrations had bolstered her confidence and prepared her for seeing Jake.

Candice and Ewan's wedding was being held in the garden of the National Wine Centre and as Scarlett made her way through the vines to the chairs placed alongside them she was glad she was wearing wedges. She and Ruby had only just found a seat when Candice's sister, who was the matron of honour, started down the aisle that had been constructed between two rows of vines.

She was accompanied by two angelic-looking children, a flower girl and page boy. Scarlett knew they weren't Candice's niece and nephew and she wondered briefly who they belonged to before her attention was diverted by the bride, who was being walked down the aisle by her father.

The ceremony was lovely, simple and straightforward but heartfelt. Scarlett always loved a good wedding, even if she couldn't quite dismiss the feeling that disaster beckoned. She crossed her fingers, hoping for the best for Candice and Ewan.

As the ceremony ended and she rose from her seat to follow the other guests back to the function centre, she searched the faces for Jake. She lost sight of Ruby as she melted into the crowd that had gathered on the outdoor terrace for pre-dinner drinks, but Scarlett didn't worry. Ruby knew a few of Candice's friends and she'd be fine. She was no shrinking violet. Scarlett had too many nerves of her own in anticipation of seeing Jake to worry about Ruby. Despite their differences, she hadn't been able to stop thinking about him. She hadn't yet found the secret to letting the idea of him go.

She finally found him. He was talking to an attractive couple who appeared to be the parents of the flower girl and page boy. He kissed the woman on the cheek. There was something familiar about her but Scarlett couldn't work out if she knew her. Jake squatted down to talk to the children. He was too far away for Scarlett to hear what he said, but his comments made them both laugh. He ruffled the boy's hair as he stood up and his movements brought Scarlett into his line of sight.

He didn't take his eyes off her and she could read his lips as he excused himself and began to walk towards her. He was wearing a light grey suit and Scarlett had a fleeting thought that this was the most dressed she'd seen him. He had a white shirt under his suit jacket and a green tie that matched his eyes. Even fully dressed, he looked gorgeous.

His walk was fluid and graceful as he crossed the terrace, collecting two glasses of champagne from a waiter as he made his way to her. Scarlett hadn't moved since their eyes had met. She was frozen to the spot, fixed in place by his eye contact, totally under his spell.

CHAPTER SIX

HE FLASHED HIS cheeky smile at her as he reached her side and that was enough to break the spell and allow her to breathe again.

'You look gorgeous.' He ran his eyes over her and Scarlett felt herself grow warm with his attention. Her make-over, courtesy of Ruby, had bolstered her confidence but not enough to prevent her from dissolving into a mass of nerves under his gaze. The make-up and hairstyle—Ruby had held her hair back with a hairband and teased it behind the band into a sixties style, letting the weight of it fall down Scarlett's back—were not protection enough against the surge of attraction she felt the moment she saw him.

'Champagne?'

Her hand shook as she accepted the glass and a shiver of excitement ran through her as his fingers brushed hers.

'Are you cold?' he asked. 'Shall we move into the sun?'

It was late afternoon and the sun was getting low in the sky, the heat losing its intensity as the day drew to an end. They were standing on the terrace in the shade of the building and Jake moved a few steps into the sunshine. Scarlett followed automatically. Her feet didn't wait for any conscious instruction—it seemed she was programmed to his frequency and she couldn't override her reaction.

'How was your day?' he asked.

Scarlett sipped her champagne as she filled him in on her day's activities and was surprised to find she'd drunk half her glass by the time she'd finished talking.

'So it's been a family affair for both of us today.'

Of course, he'd been talking to his sister—that was why the woman had looked familiar. Their faces were a similar shape, although his sister's was more heart-shaped, less of a pentagon, less angular than Jake's.

'That was your sister you were talking to earlier? Were the flower girl and page boy your niece and nephew?'

Jake nodded. 'That's Mary and her husband, Ted.'

'Are the rest of your family here?'

'Evangeline is. My brothers aren't and my other sister, Ruth, lives in the States. Her first baby is due any day now and my parents have gone over to help her.'

'That's a big family. What number are you?'

'Two older brothers, three older sisters, then me.'

Scarlett smiled as aspects of Jake's personality fell into place. 'That's why you're so relaxed, you're the baby. I bet there was always someone looking out for you and you've never had to worry about anything.'

'And I bet you're the eldest sibling.' Jake grinned. There was no malice in his voice, just laughter. His green eyes sparkled and Scarlett basked in his attention. 'You would always be complaining that the rest never had it as tough as you and that the younger ones all got away with murder.'

In Scarlett's case it was true. She wondered if the lack of responsibility her sisters seemed to feel was due simply to their personalities or also to their birth order. She knew of several studies that indicated that birth order had a lot of influence over personality and she didn't begrudge her sisters, but sometimes she wished she could experience what it felt like to be carefree, instead of constantly thinking about her responsibilities and worrying about doing the right thing. But she knew Jake's comment had been made in jest. As accurate as he was, she was sure he wouldn't really want to know how tough her childhood and her early years in particular had been.

'So you're number one and Ruby is number two?' he asked, and when Scarlett nodded he added, 'Which one is she?' But before she could answer he changed his mind. 'No, don't tell me, I'll see if I can guess.'

'Good luck.' Scarlett laughed.

'I assume by that you mean you don't look alike?'

The champagne had taken the edge off her nerves and she laughed and raised one eyebrow and replied, 'I'll let you be the judge of that.'

'If I guess right, what will you give me?'

She had no idea and when he looked at her as though he wanted to devour her she was too scared to ask what he wanted.

'Can't decide?' Jake grinned, laughing at her with his green eyes and making her stomach flutter. 'Don't worry, I'll think of something.'

His cheeky bravado made her accept his challenge, confident he'd never be able to pick out Ruby. With a tilt of her head and a slight smirk she agreed. 'Okay, go for it.'

He scanned the crowd, commenting on the different women and why they couldn't be Ruby. He had a

practised eye but his comments weren't offensive, they
were simply entertaining.

'You're supposed to be telling me which one *is* Ruby,
not which ones aren't,' Scarlett teased.

'She's the blonde over there, wearing the blue top
and no bottoms.' Jake nodded towards Ruby, picking
her out without hesitation.

Scarlett laughed at his description, it was exactly
what she would have said, but she was amazed that he'd
got it right. 'How did you know?'

'I could tell by her legs.' He looked back at Scarlett
before lowering his eyes and running his gaze down
her bare legs. The heat in his gaze stirred the pool of
desire in her belly and she could feel it spread through
her. 'You have the same legs,' he told her.

Self-consciously Scarlett tugged at the hem of her
dress, trying desperately to make it longer as she fought
the tide of desire.

'Don't,' he remonstrated. 'You have fabulous legs,
you should show them off.'

Scarlett blushed, wondering if he could see the effect he had on her or whether the make-up hid her discomfort. His green gaze held hers and his cheeky smile
curled the corners of his mouth. She had to look away
before she gave in to a crazy notion and leant forward
to taste his lips. She looked across the terrace, away
from temptation, and her gaze met Ruby's.

Ruby's ears must have been burning. She was looking directly at them and was now coming their way.
Scarlett felt a flutter of panic. She didn't want to introduce them. She didn't want Jake to fancy Ruby and in
her experience men always did. She didn't want Jake to
be like all the others. She knew she was being hypocritical and selfish and she also knew that if Ruby wanted

Jake there'd be precious little she could do to stop her, but she wasn't going to stand by and facilitate a meeting. She needed to keep them apart for as long as possible.

As she was deciding on a course of action the flower girl came running up to them, crashing into Jake's knees and distracting Scarlett.

'Papa is coming to pick us up, I have to say good-bye,' she said, as Jake swung her up to sit on his hip.

While he was busy with his niece Scarlett saw the perfect opportunity to make an escape and headed Ruby off at the pass. She touched Jake's shoulder. 'I'll catch up with you later,' she said, knowing he was too busy to stop her.

She intercepted Ruby halfway across the terrace. She tucked her arm into her sister's and guided her over to a drinks waiter.

'Hot guy. Who is he?' Ruby said, as she glanced back to where Jake was still conversing with his niece.

'He's a friend of Candice's.'

'I don't remember her having friends like that when we worked together.'

'He's from Adelaide.'

'That's okay.' She shrugged. 'Is he single?'

'As far as I know.'

'I might have to meet him later.'

Scarlett knew her little interception wouldn't be enough to stop Ruby. Ruby wouldn't wait for an introduction, she'd introduce herself. It was yet another difference between them. She needed to go to the bathroom but she didn't dare leave Ruby alone. She knew the first thing she'd do would be to head for Jake. Scarlett lifted a glass of champagne and a non-alcoholic cider from the waiter's tray before steering Ruby towards Mel. She'd make her keep an eye on Ruby for the time being.

She handed them each a glass, champagne for Mel and cider for Ruby, and said, 'I'm just going to the loo.' She ducked inside the restaurant and almost knocked over the seating plan that was displayed on a board by the main doors. She looked it over quickly. She found her name on table six. Ruby's name was there too. And so was Jake's.

She scanned the room for table six and when she found it she detoured past to check the place settings on her way to the bathroom. She circled the table, looking for her name. She found Ruby's first. To her left was Jake. To Jake's left was her own name.

Candice had put Jake between her and Ruby.

She couldn't think of a worse situation. She couldn't possibly sit next to him all through dinner but she didn't want Ruby next to him either. She picked up her name card before putting it back down. Who should she move? She couldn't move both of them so which one should it be?

Her nerves wouldn't stand being seated next to Jake. She'd have to move herself. She picked up her place card again and switched it with that of another girl at the table, a nurse from the hospital, who she knew was single. Maybe *she* could distract Jake from Ruby.

Scarlett was trying to relax and make the best of the situation she'd created when she'd moved her place setting. Her manoeuvring had resulted in her sitting between one of the groom's friends, Simon, and Jake's brother-in-law, Ted. While both men seemed perfectly nice, and Scarlett knew this would be a good opportunity to pump Ted for information about Jake, she was having huge trouble concentrating on their conversation. Her meddling had positioned her opposite Jake and now she had a bird's-eye view of Jake and Ruby. They were deep in discussion, a discussion she was desperate to overhear, but the noise level in the room meant that was impossible.

She realised too late that what she should have done was switch Jake's name card. That way neither she nor Ruby would have been sitting next to him and she still would have only moved one person. But that hadn't oc-curred to her until now and what's done was done. She would just have to live with the consequences.

From what she could see, Ruby and Jake appeared to be getting on famously. It was what she had been afraid of and it wasn't surprising. Ruby had a lot of her father in her—he was extremely charismatic and was always the life of the party—but she would hate to know that her sister was comparing her to him because he was also a liar and a cheat, two things Ruby definitely wasn't.

Maybe Ruby was more Jake's type, Scarlett thought. She definitely danced to the beat of her own drum and did whatever she pleased, creating her own fun, much like Scarlett suspected Jake did. She sighed and let Ted refill her glass as she resigned herself to the fact that she couldn't control the world and she definitely couldn't control Jake and Ruby. If they were kindred spirits she should be wishing them luck.

She turned her head and tried her best to ignore Jake as she made an effort to engage Simon in conversation while she picked at her dinner. The food looked deli-cious and she was almost certain it was, but seeing Ruby and Jake together had ruined her appetite.

By the time her main-course plate had been cleared away Candice and Ewan were on the dance floor, dancing their version of the bridal waltz. Slowly the guests began to join the bride and groom. From the corner of her eye Scarlett saw Jake rising from his seat. Involuntarily, she turned her head, expecting to see him ask Ruby to dance, but his eyes were fixed on hers as he made his way around their table to her side.

'Dance with me?' His voice poured over her, softening her resistance with its treacle tones. His green eyes had her fixed in his sights, making her forget where they were and who he was. She couldn't concentrate when he looked at her like that, as if he wanted to consume her, as if she was the only woman in the room. Just a look from him now and she was ready to self-combust. Just a look and she could recall the touch of his fingers on her skin, the warmth of his lips on hers, the weight of his body between her thighs. Her body responded to his gaze and she felt the heat pooling in her groin.

As if he could read her thoughts, the corners of his mouth lifted into a smile that was just for her. He was holding out one hand to help her from her seat. It was hard to resist and automatically she put her hand in his. Her skin came alive as his fingers closed around hers. The heat in her belly raced through her and joined with the fire in her fingertips and her heartbeat quickened as her body came to life.

But as her body woke up, so did her brain. Touching him was enough to make her come to her senses. 'No.' She snatched her hand back, as though she'd been burnt. 'I can't.'

She couldn't imagine being held in his arms while everyone else watched. She couldn't imagine being able to keep her feelings under control while his hands were on her skin, while she could feel his breath on her cheek, while they danced in front of a crowd. It was too dangerous. She'd almost made a big mistake.

'I'll dance with you.'

Scarlett's heart lodged in her throat as she heard Ruby's invitation and Jake's acceptance and it stayed there, making breathing almost impossible as she had to sit and watch and smile while Jake danced with Ruby. While he held Ruby in his arms.

Her hand shook as she poured herself a glass of water and lifted it to her lips. She swallowed hard, forcing the liquid past the lump in her throat. She needed to get a grip on her emotions. She couldn't let him affect her like this. Why did he upset her equilibrium so massively? This reaction was so unlike her. She wanted him but she knew she couldn't have him. She needed to forget about Jake. He could dance with whoever he pleased, it couldn't matter to her.

But she still wished it didn't have to be Ruby.

Ruby had been waiting to get Jake alone and out of earshot of the rest of the table. There were things she needed to ask him. Like what was going on between him and Scarlett. He'd told her he was a med student and that he was doing a placement in Emergency with Scarlett, a rather interesting piece of information that Scarlett had neglected to tell her, and Ruby wanted to know why. She had seen them on the terrace during the pre-dinner drinks and she remembered Scarlett's expression. It had been clear to her that Scarlett only had eyes for Jake—she had been completely unaware of anyone else but him.

She had baited Scarlett earlier, teasing her about meeting Jake, wanting to see if Scarlett let any info slip, but she played her cards close to her chest, just as she'd always done. But it was obvious to Ruby that Scarlett liked Jake and she wanted to know if her sister's feelings were reciprocated.

Jake held her right hand in his left and she could feel his right palm pressing into the small of her back. The pressure was firm enough just to let her know that he knew what he was doing. He had nice strong arms and a good frame and she relaxed and let him lead her around the dance floor.

'Now that we're alone, are you going to tell me what's going on between you and my sister?'

'I don't know what you're talking about.' He avoided her gaze as he spun her out of the way of another couple who looked fairly clueless.

'I'm talking about the fact that neither of you could keep your eyes off each other all through dinner yet you behaved as though you were strangers. Why didn't you move around the table and talk to her? Why were you ignoring her?'

'Because she wants me to.' His gaze was direct this time.

'How do you know?'

'I asked Candice to put Scarlett next to me at the table,' Jake told her, 'and I assume she did, there was no reason not to, yet Scarlett was sitting opposite me. She must have moved place settings to avoid me.'

'Why would she do that? What have you done to her?'

'Nothing. But I think I make her uncomfortable.'

'Because she likes you?'

'Yes,' he admitted. 'But not enough.'

'You should ask her out.' Ruby could never see the point of hanging back. If she wanted something she went and got it, and she figured more people should live by that philosophy.

'I have.'

'Really?'

'Yep.'

'And…?'

'She turned me down. She says she can't date a student. Apparently it's unethical.'

'She's probably right,' Ruby said. 'She's a bit of a stickler for the rules. But surely she's allowed to dance with you tonight?'

'I believe she is.'

'So why isn't she?'

'She doesn't know what to do with me. I don't think I fit into any of her neat little boxes. I suspect she feels I might cause chaos in her orderly world.'

'So what are your plans? You obviously like her too. Are you just going to keep ignoring her or are you going to ask her out again?'

Jake was laughing.

'What?'

'I feel like I'm dancing with one of my sisters. They like to boss me around as well.'

'Well, it sounds as though you need it.'

'Then you'll be pleased to know that I do have a plan. I thought I'd let her have a few more glasses of champagne before I ask her to dance again. She likes me better when she's had a few drinks,' he explained.

'Is that so?'

'Yep. I'll wait for her to relax a bit more and then hopefully she'll be up for some fun.'

'Can I give you some advice?' she asked.

'About Scarlett?'

Ruby nodded.

'Sure.'

'She's not really about having fun. She takes life very seriously.'

'I've learnt that but I'd like to see if I can change her mind. Show her how to have a good time.'

Ruby grinned at him. She suspected that would be something he'd be very good at but she thought it only fair to warn him. 'You'll need to take things slowly. She's not very good at letting people into her world. She's cautious. She expects people to let her down, men in particular. She doesn't like to rely on anyone but herself. For anything.'

'That's okay, I'm not in any hurry. I can do slow.'

Scarlett felt as though she'd been watching Jake dance for hours. He was a good dancer and watching him was certainly no hardship, but watching the succession of partners was becoming tedious.

She wished she hadn't felt so self-conscious, she wished she could trust herself to keep her emotions in check, she wished she could have danced with him. The dance floor was crowded now; she was probably more conspicuous sitting alone at the table than she would be if she was in Jake's arms. He danced confidently. He was light on his feet and had good rhythm. He'd looked like he didn't have a care in the world as he'd danced with Ruby, his sisters, Mel, several of the nurses, Candice—she'd been keeping a mental tally— and now with Diana.

He had removed his suit jacket and she could see the muscles in his butt, back and shoulders flex and relax as he guided Diana around the floor. If he asked her to dance again she'd say yes, she decided. Surely one dance couldn't hurt.

She followed his path around the dance floor, her eyes glued to the crisp brightness of his white shirt, her eyes straining as she tried to see if his tattoo was visible through the thin fabric. He hadn't so much as glanced her way since he'd taken to the dance floor and she felt safe to study him, knowing he was unlikely to catch her out.

She found his tattoo fascinating. She felt as if it was their secret, even though she knew any number of other women had probably seen it but she refused to let her mind dwell on that. She wanted to feel as though they had shared something special. She knew they weren't likely to share anything else, but she could still close her eyes and recall tracing her fingers over the tattooed stars. It would be her memory. One no one could take away.

He lifted his left arm and spun Diana under and away from him and Scarlett's eyes immediately flicked to the inside of his upper arm, to the junction of his biceps and triceps muscles, to see if she could spy the stars. As she searched for the shadow of the Southern Cross she heard someone pull out the chair next to her and guiltily she looked away from Jake to find Richard sitting down beside her.

'Richard! How are you feeling?'

'Surprisingly fit and well. I really feel as though I have a new lease of life.'

She studied him properly for the first time in weeks. He'd aged in that time but it wasn't all that surprising. He'd lost weight but he didn't look too thin, and the fact that he'd lost his tan after stopping his weekly golf game was probably to blame. He was a good-looking man, she acknowledged, but he certainly didn't take her breath away and make her insides go all gooey like Jake did.

She realised now she had never had that same intensity of reaction to Richard. Had he ever turned her knees to jelly? She didn't think so. But she'd been happy. Or maybe just not *unhappy*.

'I came over to apologise. Diana told me you knew she was going to invite me to come to the wedding with her but I hope it hasn't put you on the spot. It wasn't my intention to make you feel uncomfortable in any way by accompanying Diana today.'

'It's not a problem,' Scarlett reassured him. 'I was happy for her to ask you.' It was far better than the alternative—that Diana had wanted to ask Jake. 'I want you to have everything you wish for and I'm sorry I couldn't give you what you wanted.' Scarlett didn't bear Richard any ill will. They weren't compatible, and maybe he could be happy with Diana.

Now that he had unburdened himself, his gaze sought out his date. 'Diana doesn't seem to be in any hurry to get off the dance floor.'

Why would she be? Scarlett thought. She was dancing with Jake.

'Shall we join them?' Richard asked.

'Are you up to it?'

'Most definitely.'

She might as well be dancing instead of sitting alone at the table. She took Richard's hand and was curious to discover that she felt nothing. There was no rush of desire, no overreacting nerve endings, no breathlessness. She fought to pay attention to Richard as he guided her around the dance floor but her body had a mind of its own and her eyes kept seeking Jake.

If she had any doubts about her decision not to marry Richard she had her answer now as her eyes found Jake. Even if she could count on Richard to be dependable and committed she knew she could never go back. Their relationship had been convenient and safe, but it had never been exciting. Jake was like a drug and she knew she could easily become addicted to the buzz she got when she was with him, to the surge of attraction and the adrenalin, and that was what she wanted now. She wanted excitement.

She kept her eyes on Jake. While she couldn't imagine being with him long term she knew what she wanted now. Adventure. Excitement. Pleasure. Richard was a good man but she wanted more than that. There was no harm in wanting, was there?

Jake and Diana were getting closer. Scarlett remembered why she didn't like dancing with a partner—men got to call the shots. Richard was guiding her around the dance floor and she had no control over where they went. Jake and Diana were right beside them now and there was nothing she could do about it.

'Shall we swap partners?' Jake asked, directing his question to Diana. Richard and Diana didn't even argue. As if the move had been rehearsed, Jake let go of Diana and she stepped into Richard's arms. Their timing gave Scarlett no option. If she hadn't let Jake take hold of her she would have been stranded in the middle of the dance floor. But as she felt his hand close over hers and the familiar flutter in her belly she thought perhaps she should have escaped while she'd had the chance. But Jake wasn't letting her go.

'I've been waiting all night to dance with you. Just one dance, can you give me that?' he asked, as if he knew she was deliberating over her options.

The band was playing a slower number now and Jake slid his hand further around her back, pulling her in close. His hand was warm against the small of her back and he positioned her so that one of her legs was tucked between his thighs and he was able to control her movements with slight pressure of his hands, his fingers and his thighs. But Scarlett didn't feel trapped or controlled. She felt like part of him. He was light on his feet and she relaxed and let him take over. She'd been wishing she could have just one dance, and this was her chance.

Her breasts were pressed against his chest and she could feel the heat of his body through his shirt. His body was hard and strong against hers. She turned her head to the right and breathed in his scent. He smelt like a summer day, fresh and warm. His left arm was outstretched and she could see the dark shadow of his tattoo through the sleeve of his shirt. She focused on the stars. She didn't need to concentrate on dancing, her body followed Jake's rhythm effortlessly. She wanted to rest her head against him and close her eyes and imagine they were alone but she had to resist and re-member where they were. She forced herself to make conversation.

'Where did you learn to dance?'

'I spent years being dragged along to my sisters' ballet classes. When I wouldn't sit still and started complaining, Mum enrolled me in classes too. Not bal-let—jazz and contemporary mainly. I loved it and I've never stopped. When I was in high school it was a good way to get the girls—girls love a boy who can dance. And it comes in handy now for my job.'

Scarlett frowned. 'For medicine?' That made no sense and she wondered if she'd drifted off and had missed part of his answer.

He shook his head and his lips lifted in a smile as he laughed. 'No, The Coop.'

'You need to be able to dance to work behind the bar?' She remembered him moving to the music but his movements had looked completely natural, albeit totally hot, but they certainly hadn't looked choreographed.

'I'm not just a barman,' he said, as he tipped her backwards into a dip and then lifted her upright again before she had a chance to complain that she was too heavy. She knew she wasn't, she knew he had total control, he was ninety per cent sexy, muscled hunk and ten per cent cheek, although she admitted she should allocate some percentage for intelligence as well.

'Sure, there's judging the contests too,' she said, once she'd recovered her equilibrium.

'Everyone at The Coop does a bit of everything.'

He paused and Scarlett wondered what he was waiting for. He had tilted his head to the side as he watched her and once again she had the sense she'd missed something but she had no idea what.

He was smiling at her as he said, 'You do realise I'm a stripper?'

'What?' Scarlett frowned, not sure if she'd heard correctly.

'A stripper,' he repeated. 'Someone who gets paid to take their clothes off in public.'

CHAPTER SEVEN

SCARLETT STOPPED DEAD in the middle of the dance floor, almost causing a collision.

'I know what a stripper is,' she said, although she still wasn't quite sure that she believed her own ears. But even while she thought her ears were deceiving her, her imagination was taking flight. Her initial reaction was completely visual. She could picture him playing the part. An image of him semi-naked, bare-footed, bare-chested and wearing only jeans was imprinted on her brain from the time they'd first met. If she closed her eyes she could picture the muscle definition of his abdominals, the smoothness of his tanned chest and the perfectly shaped stars of his tattoo. She could imagine him on stage wearing nothing but a cheeky grin and tiny leather shorts, lapping up the attention.

Her heart was racing at the mental picture she had created until she suddenly wondered if he was pulling her leg. She searched his face, looking for a tell-tale grin. She narrowed her eyes and watched him carefully as she asked, 'Is that really what you do?'

'Of course.' She could see no sign of a smirk accompanying his reply. 'What did you think I did there?' he asked as he steered her to the side of the dance floor, making sure they weren't going to get trampled.

'I thought you worked behind the bar.'

'I do but we're jacks of all trades. We're bar staff, waiters, strippers.'

He really wasn't kidding and she had no idea what to do with this new information. She wasn't sure if she should be shocked or intrigued, horrified or excited.

'You really didn't know?' he asked.

Gradually she became aware that they were still standing on the edge of the dance floor. She took his arm and almost dragged him outside to the terrace. She was not going to have this conversation around other people. How would she ever explain sleeping with a student *and* a stripper? She breathed a sigh of relief as he followed her outdoors.

Thank God no one knows we slept together, she thought, and she intended to keep it that way.

'Of course I didn't know,' she told him, as she checked their surroundings to make sure they were alone. 'Do you think I would have slept with you if I'd known?'

'You tell me. You didn't seem to have too many res-ervations. You didn't seem that interested in the finer details.'

She knew he was right. She'd wanted to do some-thing out of character and she hadn't seen any reason to find out too much about him. She'd simply been look-ing for a physical connection, not a deep and mean-ingful conversation. In fact, she'd deliberately avoided any personal discussion. She'd been tempted by a hot stranger and she'd been more than happy to let him scratch an itch for her.

Her anger, which she knew stemmed from surprise and embarrassment, subsided. It was hardly his fault that she was naïve. It was hardly his fault she hadn't asked any questions, let alone the right ones.

'You're right. I'm sorry,' she apologised. 'I didn't stop to think. I didn't want to know anything about you really, other than what I could see. I wanted to pretend I was someone else, someone who was used to having a good time.'

'Well, that's my job. To make sure people have a good time.'

Just how good a time was he talking about? Was that what he'd been doing for her? And how many women had been there before her? She felt a blush steal across her throat and embarrassment made her words stick to the roof of her mouth. 'Do you—? Are you—?'

Jake shook his head. He obviously got the gist of her half-asked question. 'No. My job stops when I leave The Coop. Anything after that is my choice, my time.'

'But you must have picked up other girls in The Coop?'

'Actually, I haven't. I make a point not to. Most of the girls in The Coop are not at their best. Drunk and loud isn't really my type.'

She wondered if she should admit to having been slightly more intoxicated than she was used to but while she'd certainly had more to drink than was usual she knew she'd been in full control. She remembered every blissful minute of that night.

'I noticed you because you were different from the usual clients but I didn't intend to sleep with you.'

'You didn't?' Scarlett blushed. Had she made a complete idiot of herself by kissing him back, inviting him in and then almost begging him to sleep with her?

'Well, not that night anyway.' He grinned and Scarlett relaxed very slightly. 'You were a friend of a friend,

I was being nice, offering to walk you to your taxi, but then…' He shrugged.

'So you take your clothes off in front of complete strangers for a living but you don't use your job to pick up women?'

'I do have some morals and it's not all my clothes. It's no different to being a life model for an art class or a patient for the surface anatomy viva in our exams. I keep more clothes on than they do and I'm paid better and it's fun. There's no harm in it. It's not illegal.'

'I couldn't do it.' Scarlett hadn't had a chance to work out what she thought about Jake being a stripper but she knew it was not something she could ever imagine doing.

He laughed and the sound lifted her spirits. She supposed in the grand scheme of things that finding out he was a stripper was hardly the worst thing that had ever happened.

'No one is asking you to,' he said. 'You were happy to join in at The Coop, though. You have to admit it's good entertainment.'

'I hated it. I was so far out of my comfort zone.'

'What did you hate? The show? The music? The atmosphere? Me?'

'No.' Definitely not him. 'Being on the stage. I had to pretend I was someone else up there. The girl you met at The Coop wasn't me.'

'The girl I met at The Coop came from somewhere.'

'I was pretending I was Ruby,' she admitted. 'I'm the nerdy, shy, clever sister who behaved completely out of character that night. You should be dancing with Ruby, I'm sure the two of you have far more in common.'

Now more than ever, Scarlett wished she was more like Ruby. Surely Jake would rather be with someone who didn't take life so seriously? She was no match for him.

'And I'd rather be out here with you,' he said, as he ran one finger along the bare skin of her forearm, leaving a trail of heat from her elbow to her wrist. Scarlett could feel her nipples tauten in response to his touch and she couldn't think of anywhere else she'd rather be either.

'It's you I want to get to know,' he told her. 'Not Ruby or anyone else.'

'Why?' Scarlett knew exactly why she had slept with Jake but she couldn't understand why he'd want to be with her.

'When I first saw you I thought you were gorgeous and sexy and then I found out you were intelligent and fun as well. I think you're fascinating and I want to see all your different layers. Not just the person you want everyone to see. Do you remember the children's party game Pass the Parcel?'

Scarlett nodded. She knew the game but she didn't have the words to tell Jake that she hadn't gone to parties when she was little. She used to be invited to them but she never told her mother because she knew they didn't have the money for a present and she didn't have a party dress. She didn't want Jake feeling sorry for her. Those days were well and truly behind her, there was no point in bringing up the past.

'You remind me of the parcel.'

She frowned. 'How?'

'You seem to have lots of different layers and I want to unwrap each one and find out what's underneath.'

'I don't have different layers. What you see is what you get. I'm not complicated or interesting. All my life I've been the responsible one, the one who doesn't cause any problems, the one who does the right thing, who worries about what other people think.'

'I disagree. The girl on stage doing the limbo, she's inside you somewhere, underneath that responsible exterior.'

Scarlett shook her head. 'I was pretending. I'm not sure I really know how to be that person and I'm not sure if I want to be. I'm not Ruby and while I admit there are times I envy her I'm not sure that I really want to be her.'

'Are you and Ruby really so different?'

'Ruby is the wild one of our family. She's the fun, outgoing one, the one who has the adventures, the one who doesn't care what people think. If that's what you want, I'm not that person. I've always chosen studying over partying. I'm not a party girl.'

'And I'm not saying you should be. I'm only saying I think there's more to you than you want people to see and I find you fascinating. I want to get to know you. The real you. The complete you. I think we'd have fun together.'

Scarlett couldn't deny that she had fun with Jake but she couldn't imagine it continuing. 'I think you'll be disappointed. I don't think we have anything in common.'

'I disagree.'

Scarlett held up one finger and proceeded to straighten her adjacent fingers as she counted off their differences. 'You work in a strip club. As a stripper. Something I was naively unaware of. You're a student at my hospital. You have a tattoo.'

Jake laughed. 'Well, I happen to think we have plenty in common.'

He gently flexed her index finger, returning it to her palm. 'We're following the same career path. We're at the wedding of a mutual friend,' he said, as the next finger went down, followed by her third finger. 'I have a very small tattoo in a very discreet spot and I seem to remember you rather liked it. And…' he grinned as he closed her fist and finished negating her argument '…you can't hold my part-time profession against me, not when you've only known about it for five minutes, and especially not when you've already slept with me.'

'But I wouldn't have slept with you if I'd known.'

'Liar.' He was leaning in close. His lips brushed her ear and his words were soft puffs of air on the sensitive skin of her neck. 'You might not have slept with me if you'd known I was a med student but you know you wanted me as much that night as I wanted you and, stripper or not, you would have had your way with me.' His hand was on her waist and he slid it around to cup her bottom, pulling her in against him so her belly was pressed into his groin. There was no need to guess what was on his mind. Her nipples hardened in response to his physical reaction, pushing against the soft silk of her underwear, and she knew he'd be able to feel them jutting into his chest. His next words confirmed her thoughts. 'You want me now, too.'

She should have been cross with him. She should have found his arrogance infuriating but she couldn't deny he was right. She did want him. More now than she had on that first night. Now that she knew how her body responded to his touch she thought there would probably always be a part of her that would want him but that didn't make it right. And it had nothing to do with him being a stripper. She just knew they were an incompatible combination. He was too different. But she couldn't deny she was drawn to him. But that just made him different and dangerous.

'Don't be mad, dance with me,' he said.

The music from the band floated through the open doors onto the terrace. They were standing behind a potted tree, partially shielded from view of the guests inside, and Scarlett knew it would be difficult to see them due to the shadows. They were alone but she had no idea how long their solitude would last. She didn't want to have any more missed opportunities tonight. She let the music wash over her as she relaxed against him and let him take control.

He kept his hand on her bottom and held her close against his body. She rested her cheek on his chest. His heart was a steady, soothing beat under her ear. She could have stayed like that for hours but the evening was nearly over. She wished she hadn't been so stubborn, she wished she had danced with him earlier. She could have spent the night in his arms instead of watching all the other women enjoying his company.

She closed her eyes as she dreamed about what might have been.

It had taken him all evening but now he had her right where he wanted her to be—in his arms. He finally had her undivided attention. They were alone, without interruptions. He was convinced he could get her to relax if he had the time. If they had no other distractions and no observers.

He had been aware of her watching him dance for most of the evening. Once again her words had contrasted with her actions. Her dark eyes with their hidden secrets had followed him around the dance floor. He shouldn't find that enticing, he should find it frustrating, but it seemed that every time she contradicted herself it only made him more interested.

He'd meant it when he'd said he found her fascinating. He'd known since the moment he'd laid eyes on her that she was a bundle of contradictions. The serious hairstyle and simple black dress paired with her sexy hip-swivelling walk and the sky-high heels. She was an intriguing mix of sexy and smart.

It had been the contrasts in her that had hooked him from that first glance. Her pouty lips were the type that should be painted red but hers had been slick with a pale pink gloss. Her full lips had promised forbidden delights but had framed a smile that had been hesitant and unsure.

She was an interesting but possibly dangerous package, just waiting for the right spark to set her off. Her performance on stage had hinted at what could be but she had confirmed his expectation later that night when she'd taken him to her bed and he'd been lost in the promise and mystery of her ever since.

He wanted to strip away her layers and discover what was hidden at each level. He had never been so quickly and utterly captivated before. Her contrasts appeared limitless and he was desperate to discover them all. He had never thought that contrariness could be so interesting.

The music stopped, although it took them both a few seconds to notice. It wasn't until they were interrupted by the sound of the emcee announcing it was time to farewell the bride and groom that they realised the band had fallen silent.

Scarlett stayed in his arms. She seemed in no hurry to move and he was more than happy for her to stay right where she was. 'I'm not ready for the night to end.'

'It doesn't have to end yet,' he said. 'Let me take you

home.' As he uttered the words he remembered Ruby's cautionary advice to take it slowly.

'And then what? We both know where that would lead.'

'Would that be so terrible?' He'd forgotten his vow to stay away. He'd forgotten he'd agreed to avoid scandal. He was completely under her spell and all he could think of was getting her out of her dress and having her long legs wrapped around him again while he tasted and explored her and learnt her secrets.

'Just think of all the fun we can have.'

'Do you have any idea how much trouble I would be in if anyone found out I was sleeping with a student?'

'It's not the first time.'

'I know. That makes it worse. Last time I could plead ignorance. What's my excuse this time?'

'My irresistible charm,' he whispered in her ear. His lips brushed against her earlobe and he could have sworn he could feel her resistance start to cave. 'I thought you wanted adventure?' he said, as he ducked his head lower and let his lips graze the edge of her jaw. 'You don't need to leave all the adventures for Ruby. I can be your adventure. The first student you seduced. The first stripper you took to your bed.'

'Seducing students and strippers isn't the sort of adventure I had in mind.' She was panting now, her words breathless.

'It's our secret. No one else needs to know.' His fingers brushed her breast, skimming across her nipple as he kissed the hollow at the base of her throat, and Scarlett moaned softly.

She tipped her head back to speak but ended up offering him her throat and he pressed his lips under her jaw over the pulse of her heart, and Scarlett only just managed to get her words out. 'You've only got two more weeks on placement. Can we wait until then?'

'Nine days.'

'What?'

'I've actually only got nine more days, not counting the weekend,' he said, as he ran his hand down her arm and hooked his fingers around hers. 'I guess I can wait that long.'

'Really?'

'Yes, really.' The way he was grinning at her made her think he'd just got what he wanted but she had no idea what that was. 'I was always prepared to wait until the end of my placement. Two more weeks of platonic friendship won't kill me. Especially if you're the prize at the end of it.'

Scarlett woke up with a start just as she felt Jake's fingers brush over her breast and trail across her stomach. Her eyes flew open and she was surprised to find herself alone in her bed. She would have sworn she wasn't dreaming. Even now her breasts ached with longing and her groin throbbed as her body refused to give up on the idea that Jake was sharing her bed.

Last night when he'd kissed the hollow at the base of her throat it had sent a spear of longing shooting from her belly to her groin and despite her concerns she'd been tempted, oh, so tempted to give in right then and there. But she'd resisted and now she was paying the price—an overactive imagination that refused to accept that Jake wasn't in her bed.

She closed her eyes as she ran her hands over her breasts. Her nipples puckered as she imagined Jake's fingers on her skin and she squeezed her knees together as the nerve centres in her erogenous zones sprang to

life. Her fantasy had left her on edge. She needed re-
lease but unless she took matters into her own hands
she wasn't going to get it. Doing it herself wasn't nearly
as much fun. She swung her legs out of bed, deciding
to head for the shower instead.

When she emerged from the shower, marginally
less frustrated, she was surprised to find Ruby in the
kitchen, pouring a glass of orange juice.

'You're up early,' Scarlett said.

'I promised Rose I'd go with her to check out the
vintage clothes market. Do you want to come with us?'

Ruby knew of Scarlett's aversion to second-hand
clothes. Vintage in her opinion was just another word
for second-hand, but she was tempted to go anyway. It
wasn't often she got a chance to spend time with both
her sisters at once. And going with them didn't mean
she had to buy clothes herself.

Before she could answer there was a knock on the
front door. 'Is that Rose?' she asked.

Ruby shook her head. 'Too early.'

Scarlett frowned and went to open the front door.

Jake was waiting there, lounging casually against
the veranda post as if he popped past every Sunday
morning.

'What are you doing here?'

'I came to collect on our bet.'

Scarlett frowned. 'We didn't have a bet.'

'Yes, we did. Yesterday. At Candice's wedding. And
I won. I correctly identified Ruby.'

'Oh,' Scarlett said, as she remembered how confident she'd been when she'd agreed to the bet. 'What's
your prize?'

He said nothing further. Just smiled his sexy smile

and Scarlett had a feeling she knew what he wanted. She held her breath.

'You and I are going to spend the day together.'

She exhaled. She had the perfect excuse. 'I can't. I'm going shopping with Ruby and Rose.'

'Tell them you've had a better offer.' He was still smiling at her.

He had an unfair advantage. Did he know what his smile did to her? She suspected he did. 'I thought we agreed to wait for two weeks?'

'This isn't a date. It's just two friends, hanging out. If it makes it any better we're going out of town. It's highly unlikely we'll bump into anyone who knows us and we're not doing anything wrong.'

When Scarlett still hesitated he added, 'You can trust me. I agreed to wait until I finished my placement before I let you seduce me again. No matter how much you beg I'm not going to let you take advantage of me. Today we are purely platonic. But before you accept my invitation I have a couple of questions for you, in the interests of full disclosure. Do you get motion sickness?'

'No.'

'Do you have a fear of roller-coasters?'

Scarlett frowned. As far as she knew, there were no roller-coasters in South Australia. Where was he planning on taking her? 'No.'

'What about confined spaces?'

She shook her head. She was afraid of being abandoned, of being unwanted, but she didn't have any, or almost any, of the usual phobias. 'Only spiders.'

'Good.'

'Where are we going?'

'Mallala.'

'Mallala?' Scarlett couldn't imagine what a small

country town, an hour north of Adelaide, had that could possibly be of interest to her. 'What are we doing there?'

'You'll find out soon enough. We'll have fun, trust me.'

Her curiosity was piqued. 'Can you wait here?' she asked. 'I'll see if Ruby lets me make an excuse.' She didn't want Jake to come in as she suspected he and Ruby would gang up on her and make her go. If she tackled them individually she might at least feel as though she was still in charge of the decision.

'Who was it?' Ruby asked.

'Jake. He's invited me to spend the day with him. He has some secret activity planned.'

'I bet he does.' Ruby's eyes were sparkling as she laughed.

'What's so funny?'

'Nothing, I'm just imagining the activity and I'm amazed either of you have lasted this long. There were enough sparks between you and Jake last night to start a bushfire. The pair of you couldn't keep your eyes off each other. I'm surprised you didn't go home with him after the wedding. You should definitely go.'

Scarlett knew what Ruby was picturing but she also knew she was wrong. Jake had promised a platonic activity and Scarlett believed him. There was no reason not to. For a start, there'd be no reason to drive to Mallala if he wanted to spend the day in bed.

'I'm not sure it's a good idea,' she said.

'Are you kidding me?' Ruby replied. 'It's a terrific idea. He's cute and hot and fun and he likes you.'

'He's also a student.'

'Pah! It's easy enough to sneak around and not get caught if you want something badly enough. If you want *him* badly enough, which I think you do.'

'We've discussed it.'

'Discussed it? What are you wasting your time talking for? Get his gear off.'

'Shh,' Scarlett said. She was very much aware of the fact that Jake was still by the open front door and could probably hear their conversation if he listened hard enough. 'You know me, I like to play by the rules and I like to have a plan.'

'Okay, let's hear this plan of yours.' Ruby was still laughing.

'We're keeping things platonic until he finishes his placement in two weeks' time.'

'Are you sure you can wait that long?'

'We'll have to.'

'And what if his next placement is back in your hospital?'

Scarlett shook her head. 'He wants to do obstetrics and everyone wants to be sent to the city because it's convenient, but it's rare that students get two plum placements in a row.'

'Two weeks is a long time.'

'For you maybe. It will give me time to work out if I really want to do this.'

'Why wouldn't you? He's sexy and cute and smart. Have some fun.'

'I'm not sure I can handle it, handle him,' Scarlett admitted. 'He's so different from my usual type.'

'He's asked you to spend a day with him, not the rest of your life,' Ruby argued. 'Maybe it's time you tried something different.'

'You don't get much more different than a stripper.'

'What?' Ruby inhaled some orange juice and then coughed, sending a spray of juice onto the kitchen bench.

'He has a part-time job at a male revue as a stripper,' Scarlett told her, enjoying the fact that she'd been able to shock Ruby for once. It wasn't often she had that opportunity.

Ruby didn't stay shocked for long. She burst into hysterical laughter. 'I knew I liked him. A naughty streak gets me every time. Have you seen his show?'

Scarlett could feel herself blushing. 'I've seen all I need to see. Thank God no one knows I slept with him.'

'You slept with him? When?'

'The night we met. Before I knew he was a med student.'

'Well, it seems you're already experiencing different as far as he's concerned. That changes everything.'

'I'd forgotten I hadn't told you and it doesn't change anything.'

'What else haven't you told me?'

'Nothing. That's it.'

'Well, that's plenty. Now, stop arguing and go and get ready before he changes his mind. I'm not leaving till tomorrow, we can have dinner with Rose tonight.'

An hour later Scarlett slid the hair elastic down her ponytail, letting it sit lower at the base of her neck to accommodate the helmet that she was about to pull on. She wriggled it into place. It was a snug fit but not uncomfortable and the padding muffled the sounds of their surroundings. Jake adjusted the chin strap and Scarlett caught her breath as his fingers brushed the soft skin of her throat.

'You're good to go.' He grinned at her as he pulled his own helmet on.

Jake had brought her to a race circuit in the middle of dry dusty paddocks, and she was about to climb into a V8 racing car for a hot lap. The car was emblazoned with advertising and even though she knew it was the same model as hundreds of family sedans that filled the roads every day it looked fast and dangerous. She wasn't convinced this was a good idea but she didn't want to back out now. She was determined to be brave. Jake had arranged this for her and she was determined to enjoy herself. She had to trust Jake not to hurt her, to keep her safe, but even she could see the irony in that.

He opened the passenger door for her and helped to strap her into the racing harness.

'Sit right back, as flat as you can against the seat,' he said, as he tightened the straps. His hands brushed across her chest as he adjusted the harness and even though she was fully clothed in a fire-retardant racing suit she would swear she could feel the heat of his hands.

Jake slid through a back window into the seat behind her as Sean, their racing driver, double-checked the harness. Scarlett wasn't surprised to find she had no reaction whatsoever to Sean's touch.

Scarlett nervously checked her surroundings. The interior of the car looked familiar, more like the family sedans she was used to, with the exception of the steering-wheel, extra roll bars, the harnesses in place of seat belts and the fire extinguisher that was positioned between her and the driver's seat. On the dashboard in front of her, in place of the glove box, was a horizontal handle. Now that she thought about it, not much was actually that familiar. She took a deep breath and steeled her nerves as Sean climbed into the driver's seat.

The V8 engine growled as he pushed the start button and the car throbbed under her. Sean gave them both a thumbs-up before pulling out of the pits and onto a start line. Scarlett could see the bank of lights at the end of the straight and Sean revved the engine as he waited for the all-clear. He was giving them the full experience. The light changed to green and Sean pushed his foot to the floor and the car shot off down the track. The power of the engine forced Scarlett back into her seat. She didn't think it was possible to sit further back, the harness was so tight to begin with, but she was definitely flattened against the backrest.

She could hear Sean changing gear as they approached the first turn. She was sure he was taking the corner too fast and she grabbed the handle in front of her with both hands, clinging on tightly—at least now she knew what the handle was for—but before she could say anything they had rounded the corner and were flying along the back straight.

Her knuckles were white and she was sure her face was too. It was terrifying. She wasn't sure yet whether it was also fun. She would reserve judgement on that.

As they approached another hairpin turn and the barrier fence loomed large in the windscreen she squeezed her eyes shut.

'It's more fun if you open your eyes.' She could hear Jake's voice and she realised the helmets must have an inbuilt communications system.

'I'm trying to keep them open but they're refusing,' she replied.

She felt the car change direction and forced her eyes open as Sean put his foot to the floor and they flew past the pits.

'Haven't we finished?' she said, as the pit buildings went by in a blur.

'Not yet. We're doing three laps.'

Another two laps! She wasn't sure she could take it. Her eyes flicked across to the dashboard as Sean came out of the hairpin at the end of the pit straight and hit the gas. She could see the speedometer—did it really read two hundred and sixty kilometres per hour?

She held on tight to the handle in front of her and concentrated on being brave. It would only be a few more minutes. She could manage.

Three minutes later she climbed out of the car on shaky legs. Jake hauled himself out through the rear window, a wide grin on his face.

'Did you enjoy that?' he asked, as he pulled his helmet off before helping her to undo hers.

'I think so.' That had been so far out of her comfort zone she wasn't sure what to think. She was normally so cautious she still wasn't sure what had convinced her to take the challenge and get into a racing car, but looking at Jake, so calm and confident, she knew it was he who had made her feel brave. He made her feel as though she could take on the world and if anything bad happened he'd be there to pick up the pieces. He was teaching her to live in the moment, not worry about the future.

'There's more to come,' he said.

'I'm not sure my heart can take more.' Scarlett wasn't just talking about the racing. Jake had tucked his helmet under his arm and he looked every inch the sexy race-car driver. How was it that he always looked to have everything under control? The wilder things got, the happier he seemed.

'Sean's going to take you out on the skid pan. And this time you get to drive.'

'What?' Scarlett turned to Sean. 'You're going to let *me* drive your racing car?'

'Don't worry, it's insured.' Sean laughed. 'And there's nothing to hit out there. Just flat dirt.'

For the next half an hour Scarlett was let loose on the

skid pan. Sean taught her how to deliberately lose control. Deliberating losing control of anything, let alone a moving vehicle, was extremely difficult for her. Her natural impulse was to hit the brakes the moment she felt the rear of the car start to slide out but when she eventually managed to follow Sean's instructions and let the car slide he then taught her to steer into the skid. Eventually she could feel the car straighten and she was able to drive out of trouble. Once she'd mastered the skid pan she felt as if she'd been given the moon.

The minute she pulled the car to a stop in front of Jake she leapt out and ran over to the fence to hug him. 'I did it! I did it! Did you see me?'

'I did. You were brilliant.' He hugged her tight and Scarlett thought this might just be the best day she'd ever had.

'That was so much fun. Thank you.' In the end she'd actually enjoyed losing control. There had been no time to worry about anything, she'd had to use all her energy to control the car and concentrate on doing what Sean told her. There'd been no time to be frightened. 'If that's what adventure is like, I'm a fan.'

'That's adrenalin.' He removed her helmet for her. 'Come on, I think you've earned a drink.' He took her hand as she thanked Sean and walked with her back to the pit buildings, only letting go of her hand to allow her to change out of her racing suit. He was waiting for her when she emerged from the change room and he handed her a soft drink before leading her to a viewing area overlooking the race track. They finished their drinks as they watched other people's laps. It looked just as fast as it had felt.

'I can't believe I actually did that,' Scarlett mused

as cars flew past them. 'How on earth did you get into this?'

'My godfather was into car racing. He started in the Car Club and I used to come out here on weekends with him. He was a doctor, a surgeon, but car racing was his passion. He taught me to give everything one hundred per cent.'

'Your car belonged to him, didn't it?' Scarlett remembered Jake telling her that on the night they'd met. The first night he'd driven her home. When Jake nodded, she added, 'Do you ever race your car?'

'No, it's not certified for racing but I still try to make it out here for car club meetings a couple of times a year. MG owners are a rather passionate, eclectic bunch. It's good fun.'

She had to agree—it *was* fun. But the best part had been spending time with Jake. He'd chosen the perfect activity. Away from the pressure of work and people they knew, taking her some place where she couldn't possibly focus on anything other than the matter at hand. There'd been no time to even think about whether spending time with him was the right or wrong thing to do. All she knew was that it felt right. Whenever she was with him she felt as though she was where she was supposed to be.

He was different but Ruby was right. Perhaps different was good. He made her happy and that certainly felt good. She was content just being in the moment when she was with him. It was unusual for her not to be worrying about work or finances or what other people expected of her. It was nice to feel relaxed.

Maybe this was how life was supposed to feel. Maybe she could be relaxed and happy and a little bit adventurous if she was with the right person. Was Jake the right person for her? Could he be?

She glanced over at him as he watched the cars zip by. He was leaning on a railing inside the protective fence and she let her eyes run over the curve of his backside. He was wearing a simple T-shirt and jeans, quite a contrast to the elegance of the suit he'd worn to the wedding and she couldn't decide how she preferred him. In a suit, in scrubs, casually outfitted or naked in her bed? He looked good in anything. And better in nothing.

She was just about to thank him again for the day when her fantasies were interrupted by terrified screams. The screams weren't coming from the racetrack but from behind them. Scarlett whipped around. The screams imparted a sense of urgency, and she saw several car tyres roll from behind one of the pit buildings and go bouncing along the ground.

Jake took off at a run and Scarlett was close behind him.

CHAPTER EIGHT

THEY ROUNDED THE corner of the building. A pile of old car tyres, which Scarlett suspected had once been neatly stacked, had collapsed, sending tyres rolling in all directions. A woman and two children were frantically tugging at what remained of the stack.

'What are you doing?'

'What's happened?' They spoke together.

'My son,' the woman panted. 'He's under here.'

Jake looked at Scarlett but only fleetingly. Before Scarlett could process what had happened Jake was hauling the tyres from the pile and tossing them to one side.

Watching Jake kicked Scarlett into action too.

'Are these also your children?' she asked the woman.

'Yes.'

'Take them around the front, into the building.' Scarlett could only imagine what grisly scene they might be about to uncover. It was better if the children were somewhere else. 'Find someone to keep an eye on them,' she told the mother, as more people arrived on the scene. Jake quickly issued instructions to the newcomers as the woman shepherded her other children out of sight but not without an anxious backward glance and Scarlett knew she'd be back as soon as possible.

Just as the on-site paramedics arrived and the boy's mother returned, Jake pulled another tyre from the stack to finally reveal the unmoving figure of a young boy. He was unnervingly still, there was not even a slight rise and fall of his chest, and Scarlett feared the worst. She introduced herself to the paramedics and gave them Jake's background as Jake bent his head to check the boy's breathing and simultaneously felt for a pulse.

'Unconscious and in respiratory arrest but he has a pulse,' Jake told the paramedics as he started mouth-to-mouth, breathing for the boy.

Who knew what other injuries he had sustained? Scarlett knew the list could be long. He could have spinal fractures, a head injury, rib fractures, a pneu-mothorax, just to name a few, but the priority was es-tablishing an airway and getting oxygen into his lungs. They worked frantically for the next few minutes.

Scarlett inserted an endotracheal tube into the boy's trachea to establish an artificial airway and once one of the paramedics was squeezing the ambu bag, forc-ing air into the boy's lungs, Jake and Scarlett helped to fit a cervical collar around his neck before transferring him onto a spinal board then a stretcher and then into the ambulance. Somehow, in the middle of the frenetic activity, Jake managed to keep chatting to the boy's mother, keeping her informed.

Scarlett breathed a sigh of relief as the ambulance raced away, lights and sirens at full strength. They had done their bit, and had done it well. Now it was up to the paramedics and the trauma team at the receiving hospital. Now that the crisis was over Scarlett found her hands were shaking. By comparison, Jake appeared remarkably unflustered if somewhat filthy from the physical exertion.

'You were unbelievably calm,' Scarlett commented, as she rubbed her hands on her arms to try to disguise her rattled nerves.

'I've been in worse situations,' he replied.

'Really? When?' Despite her recent weeks in the Emergency department Scarlett had never felt under the same sort of pressure that she had been under just then. Working in the middle of nowhere with very limited resources was an entirely new experience for her. When would Jake have experienced worse?

'I spent some time travelling around Asia during my gap year. I was travelling from Vietnam to Thailand when Cyclone Nargis hit Myanmar. The whole area became the true definition of a disaster zone. I volunteered with a charity and what I experienced there was life-changing. I had put med school on hold while I travelled and while I wasn't qualified to give any medical care I volunteered to help in the hospital.

'There were plenty of jobs assisting the medicos for anyone who wasn't squeamish and there were plenty of emergencies and terrible injuries. It was tragic and truly dreadful but any little thing anyone could do could make a difference so it was hugely rewarding at the same time, and it confirmed for me that medicine was what I wanted to do.'

Jake was constantly surprising her. He was far more mature and multi-faceted than she had given him credit for, which made him even more intriguing.

'I had no idea,' she said, but her teeth were chattering and her words weren't very clear. She rubbed her arms again, trying to stop the shaking.

Jake wrapped an arm around her shoulders. 'Come on, let's get you warm and home.' She knew the shivering was an after-effect of the adrenalin but she kept quiet. She didn't want to give Jake a reason to remove his arm. It was comforting. It was perfect. 'There won't be any more racing happening while the ambulance is gone.'

Jake opened the boot of his car, pulled out his leather jacket and helped her into it. He glanced down at his filthy T-shirt. 'This has seen better days,' he said. He whipped it off, treating Scarlett to one of her favourite views—his naked torso, abdominal muscles and tattoo. A familiar surge of longing rushed through her and she wasn't surprised to find that the heat of her reaction counteracted the adrenalin and she stopped shaking.

She was tempted to break her agreement. She was tempted to throw herself at him right then and there, but unfortunately Jake swapped the dirty T-shirt for a clean hoodie that he found in the boot and removed temptation from under her nose.

Disappointed, she climbed into his car. The end of his placement couldn't come soon enough for Scarlett.

One more day.

Less than twelve hours really until she and Jake would be free.

For the past eight days he had been leaving little notes for her, counting down the days. Yesterday he'd managed to tape an envelope to her locker. Inside had been a note that had simply said: *One more day.* The day before that she'd found a sticky note inside a patient's file that had read: *Two days to go.* Today she'd gone into the operating theatre and found an invitation on the whiteboard.

Med students dinner tonight, 7.30, Casa Barcelona. All invited.

Underneath it was a postscript that read: *Only twelve more hours*. She recognised the handwriting and she knew Jake had been in early and left the note for her. She wiped the postscript off before anyone else saw it but she was smiling and his note put her in a good mood that lasted all day.

One more day had become twelve more hours, which had now become a matter of minutes.

Scarlett checked the clock on the theatre wall as she hummed along to Richard's MP3. The final surgery for her shift was almost finished and even the nasty injury sustained by the victim of a dog attack couldn't dampen her enthusiasm and love of life today.

She hadn't wanted to go to the dinner, she'd had other plans for Jake, but he'd talked her round and she smiled as she walked through the restaurant doors as she remembered what he'd said earlier in the day. 'You need to eat, you'll need your strength.'

They'd ordered shared platters from the tapas menu for the group, and although the food was still coming Scarlett had eaten enough. She was getting edgy. She'd done the right thing, joined in the end-of-placement celebration but now she wanted to get on with the rest of the evening. Jake was sitting beside her on the long wooden bench, his thigh was pressed against hers, and she could feel the heat coming off his body and smell his freshly showered scent. She'd had enough of sitting there politely, pretending to be interested in the conversation and trying to ignore her raging hormones. She wanted to take Jake home, strip him of his clothes and take him to her bed.

She was wondering how she could suggest to him that it was time to leave without being overheard when talk moved onto the students' next placements. They had been informed of their next hospitals just that afternoon and despite her plans she was keen to hear where they were all going.

'You're doing obstetrics, Jake?' someone asked. 'Where are you going?'

'Mount Gambier.'

Scarlett's heart dropped in her chest. He was going to the country.

He must have seen her expression because he stood up from the table without adding anything further. He turned to her and held out his hand as the band started to play. 'Time for dancing,' he said.

She stood too, accepting his invitation. This would give them a chance to talk in private.

'Mount Gambier! That's five hours away,' she said as soon as they were on the dance floor. 'Couldn't you have got somewhere closer?'

'It's a great placement and I'll be the only obstetric student so I should get to do more deliveries than if I was sharing the load with other students,' he said, and she knew she was being selfish. He was right, the placement was important and a good hospital would make all the difference. 'I hear that Annie runs a really good programme,' he added, as he dipped her.

'Annie?'

'Dr Annie Simpson. She's the ob-gyn.' He was grinning at her now. 'There's no need to be jealous, she's way too old for me.'

'How old?'

'Early thirties.'

'Hey, I'm almost thirty.'

'I know,' he said, as he spun her away from him. 'I'm

just stirring you. I have everything I want right here,' he said, as he pulled her back into his arms.

Scarlett had no idea what dance they were doing but she didn't care. She didn't need to worry about the steps, she just had to follow Jake's lead.

'I know this isn't what we were hoping for,' he told her, 'but we've got a couple of days before I go so I suggest we make the most of our time and get out of here.'

'You want to leave together?'

'I thought that was the general idea. Tell you what, why don't I leave? Everyone will assume I'm going to work at The Coop. I'll grab a taxi and meet you out the front in ten minutes. You can make an excuse and join me. Okay?'

Scarlett nodded. 'That's a better plan.'

'You're not the only one with a plan,' he said, with a grin that melted her insides.

Scarlett rolled over in bed and stretched. She was still half-asleep and she could have quite happily stayed in bed for the day if she didn't have to go to work. The pillow next to her still had an indentation from Jake's head, from where he'd lain beside her for the night. She buried her face in the pillow and breathed in his scent.

She lifted her head when she heard him come into the room. He was freshly showered but only half-dressed. He had his pants on but she was treated to a fine view of his lean, well-defined torso, his ripped abdominals and a glimpse of his tattoo as he put a cup of coffee on her bedside table. He bent a little further and kissed her on the lips before reaching for his shirt and pulling it over his head. He grabbed his car keys and tossed them in the air, then caught them again. It seemed as though his good mood was a match for hers.

'I won't be able to see you tonight, I have a late lecture and then I have to work at The Coop,' he said as he slipped his feet into his shoes.

'You could come past after work,' she suggested.

'It'll be late.'

'That's okay. You can wake me up when you get here.'

'Sounds good,' he said, as he flashed his cheeky grin. His green eyes were alight as he leant over and kissed her a second time before ducking out of the door. She heard the front door open and then close.

In two days he'd be leaving for Blue Lake Hospital in Mt Gambier and she wanted to make the most of the little time they had together before he left. She smiled as she thought about last night. Their time together might be limited for the next month but if last night was anything to go by, they would be able to make the most of any spare moments. She stretched again and sat up, reaching for her coffee cup.

The sudden movement made her feel a little light-headed and a wave of nausea hit her as she inhaled the strong odour of the coffee. She put the coffee back on the table, deciding to leave it until after her shower. She spent far too long in the shower, leaving herself no time for breakfast, and she left for work with the coffee sitting untouched by her bed. She grabbed a take-away coffee and a cinnamon scroll from the cafeteria but her stomach protested over that combination of flavours too.

She put her breakfast down on a bench in the change room as she prepared to get changed into her scrubs.

She looked up as the door swung open to admit Mel.

'Are you all right?' Mel asked, as she took one look at her.

'Yep, just tired, I think. It's making me feel a little off.'

'You look dreadful. Are you hungover?'

'No.' She wasn't hungover, she'd barely touched any alcohol last night—she hadn't needed to. She'd got by on pure adrenalin. The excitement of being able to go home with Jake without feeling guilty, even if they still didn't tell anyone else what they were doing, had been enough of a buzz. She hadn't needed to drink, not when she'd had Jake.

Scarlett hadn't said anything to Mel about Jake yet. It was early days and she wanted to keep whatever happened under wraps for now, just between the two of them for a little longer. 'I think it must be something I ate last night.'

'Are you going to eat that?' Mel nodded at Scarlett's coffee and scroll, which were on the bench beside her.

Scarlett looked at her breakfast. She'd taken the scroll out of its bag but even the thought of eating or drinking anything was enough to make her feel ill. She shook her head. 'No. It's all yours.'

She bent forward to step into a pair of surgical trousers as Mel picked up the scroll and bit into it. The smell of cinnamon wafted over Scarlett. She wasn't sure if it was the smell or the position she was in but she felt decidedly woozy. She straightened up, hoping that would clear her head. 'I'm not feeling—'

Scarlett looked around her. The room looked different but it took her a moment to realise it was because she was lying on the floor. The cinnamon scroll was next to her with a bite out of it. She frowned. She didn't remember eating the scroll. And what was she doing on the floor?

'Scarlett? Can you hear me?'

She turned her head and winced as a stabbing pain shot from the back of her head into her eye socket. Mel was kneeling on the floor beside her. 'What happened?'

'You fainted.'

She frowned. 'But I never faint.'

'Okay, you passed out. Are you hurt?'

'I don't think so.'

She struggled to sit up but Mel put a hand out to stop her.

'Stay there. If you're not hurt I still want to take your BP before you go anywhere.'

Mel ducked out of the change room and came back seconds later with a sphygmomanometer. She wrapped the cuff around Scarlett's arm before inflating it. 'Ninety over sixty. What is it normally?'

'One-ten on eighty,' Scarlett replied. 'I'm fine.'

'You need to eat something.'

They both looked at the cinnamon scroll lying on the floor. 'Not that.' Mel laughed.

'Eating is what got me into this state,' Scarlett told her. 'I think if I eat anything I'll throw up.'

'Shall I run a drip for you instead?'

Scarlett shook her head, wincing again as the movement made her head throb. 'I'm not hungover and I haven't been vomiting. I don't think I'm dehydrated. I just feel off. I'm sure it's just a slight dose of food poisoning or maybe a food allergy of some sort.'

'Could be gastro. Are you having any stomach cramps?' Mel asked, as she took Scarlett's temperature. 'Your temperature's normal. No headaches?'

'I have one now,' Scarlett said as she gingerly touched

the bump on the back of her head. 'But I didn't have one before.'

Mel shrugged. 'Okay, you can skip the drip and get up, but only if you agree to go straight home and have plenty of fluids when you get there and something to eat when you can.'

'Just give me a minute, I'll be fine.'

'You need to go home in case it develops into something that could be contagious.'

'I'm sure it's just something I ate,' she protested.

'Maybe. But you did just faint. You shouldn't be at work.'

'Fine.' She felt too drained to argue and the bump on her head was throbbing.

'I'll call past after work and see how you are.'

Scarlett couldn't remember the last time she'd spent the day on the couch. She had an afternoon sleep and woke up feeling like her old self, other than the lump on the back of her head. She put the whole episode down to a lack of sleep, a chilli overload with the tapas menu and no breakfast. Thinking of food made her realise she was actually hungry. She put some bread into the toaster and flicked the kettle on for a cup of tea, thinking it still might be advisable to steer clear of coffee for a little longer.

Mel arrived as she was finishing off the first piece of toast.

'Good, you're eating. Are you feeling better?'

'I'm almost back to normal. I told you it was just something I ate.'

'I know you did but I checked and no one else who was at the restaurant last night is sick,' Mel said, as she dumped her handbag on the kitchen table and rummaged through it. 'I brought you something,' she said, pulling something from her bag.

In her hand she held a pregnancy test kit.

Scarlett stared at the box. 'Why on earth would I be pregnant?'

'You're probably not but you don't have a hangover, you didn't have a temperature or a headache or stomach pain and no one else has been sick. You're just feeling a little off and you haven't been eating.'

'I'm eating now.'

'Have you had a coffee today?'

Scarlett shook her head. 'I've made a couple but I can't stand the smell.'

'When was your last period?'

'Jeez, would you give it a rest?' Scarlett was getting nervous now.

'Well? Do you remember?'

'I'd have to check my diary.'

Mel handed her the test kit. 'Just do me a favour. Take the test and then we can cross that off the list as well.'

Scarlett sighed and snatched the kit from Mel before storming off to the bathroom. There must be a dozen different ailments she could have. Why on earth would she be pregnant? *How* could she be pregnant?

She opened the box and checked the instructions before weeing on the stick. She sat on the toilet and waited, calculating dates in her head while she waited for the time to elapse. She didn't need to check her diary. Her last period had been due on the day of Candice's wedding ten days ago and she realised now that it hadn't come. She'd been too busy at work, too busy thinking about Jake, to notice.

What if Mel was right?

She felt her stomach start to heave and knew she wasn't going to be able to keep the toast down. She stood up from the toilet, flipped open the lid and vomited into the bowl until her stomach was empty.

She rinsed her mouth and spat into the basin. The stick was sitting on the edge of the basin, daring her to pick it up.

Her hand shook as she lifted it from the sink and took it out to Mel.

She nodded at Mel's handbag. 'Do you have another one of these in there?'

'Why? Didn't it work?'

'I hope not. It's positive.'

'Oh, my God. You're pregnant!' Mel jumped out of her chair.

'No. I can't be.' Scarlett shook her head. 'That's why I need to do another test.'

Mel held her hand out. 'Let me see.' She looked at the window and Scarlett knew what she'd see. Two pink lines. 'You really are pregnant.'

Scarlett collapsed onto the couch. She'd been hoping that Mel would tell her she was seeing things. Seeing pink lines that weren't really there. 'What am I going to do? I don't want a baby.'

If she didn't want children that were planned, what on earth was she supposed to do with an unexpected baby?

'Richard will be over the moon. You don't have to worry about doing this on your own.'

'I doubt that very much.'

'You told me he wants kids. You told me that's why you broke up.'

'It might not be his.'

'What?' Mel's expression would have been funny

if the situation wasn't so dire. 'Whose could it be?' she asked.

Scarlett buried her face in her hands. 'God, what a bloody mess.' She took a deep breath. 'I slept with Jake.'

'Oh, my God. When?'

'Candice's hen's night.' She wasn't about to admit to last night's dalliance as well. 'Before I knew who he was. Well, before I knew he was a med student.'

'Oh, my God!' Mel repeated. 'What happened?'

'Remember he offered to walk me to the taxi? When we got to the street there was a huge queue for cabs so he offered to give me a lift home. One thing led to another.'

'Jeez, that was fast work. Candice was right when she said he was a charmer. Didn't you practise safe sex?'

'Of course we did. But something must have gone wrong.'

'So when you said you "can't" be pregnant, you actually could be, you just don't want to be?'

'There's no way I'm having kids, especially not on my own. And I can't imagine that Jake would want to be a father at this point in time either.'

'It doesn't have to be his, does it?'

'What do you mean?

'Is there a chance it could Richard's?'

Scarlett shook her head. 'No.' She was almost certain it wasn't Richard's.

'Well, there's always more than one option but you don't have to work it all out tonight. It's still very early days and anything could happen. If you really don't want it, maybe that's what you should hope for.'

Scarlett didn't know if she could wish for it all to go away. Not if she really was pregnant. But Mel was right, it was early days and she needed more confirmation than a home pregnancy test. The best she could hope for was that this was a mistake and all she was really suffering from was a bad case of gastro.

'Are you going to be okay? Would you like me to stay the night?' Mel asked.

'No. I'll be fine.'

Scarlett doubted she'd be fine but she'd got herself into this mess and she didn't expect Mel to have to help her sort it out. She'd figure it out one way or another but she needed a bit of time to process what had just happened. She sent Jake a quick message saying she wasn't feeling well and not to come past tonight. She hated to put him off but she needed time and space. She couldn't deal with seeing him just yet.

She was mortified. She had always tried to do the right thing, always tried to behave and avoid trouble. Her sisters constantly did as they pleased while she tried not to cause anyone grief. Most of the time her sisters got away with their behaviour and it was typical of her luck that the one time she did something out of character, the one time she was spontaneous or, dare she say irresponsible, she got into trouble.

She was always the one who helped others. Was she now going to be the one in need of help? And who would she turn to? Her mother? Jake?

If she was pregnant, she was ninety-nine per cent certain it was Jake's. But expecting support from him wasn't fair, he hadn't asked to be a father. Oh, why couldn't the baby be Richard's? At least then she would know the father wanted to be involved, but of course it couldn't be that simple.

She pulled her diary from her bag and double-checked her dates. As she'd suspected, her last period had started four weeks *before* Candice's wedding.

Almost six weeks ago. She was ten days late. She was never late.

She hadn't slept with Richard since well before that but she'd slept with Jake almost four weeks ago. It had to be his.

Mel was hovering outside Emergency the next morning, waiting for Scarlett when she arrived at work. 'How are you feeling?'

'I'm okay.'

'Have you eaten?'

Scarlett nodded. She'd swapped coffee for tea and a piece of buttered toast and so far she'd managed to keep her breakfast down.

'Have you worked out what you're going to do?' Mel asked. 'What you're going to tell Jake?'

'Nothing yet. I want to get the test confirmed first. It still could be a mistake.'

'You mean to tell me you haven't done another home pregnancy test just to see?'

'Of course I have.' She'd gone to the pharmacy last night after Mel had left and bought three more tests, all different brands, hoping one of them would give her a different answer.

'And?'

'They were all positive.' It was starting to look like she was going to have to deal with it.

'You know as well as I do that any official test is just a variation on weeing on the stick at this stage,' Mel said, effectively negating Scarlett's reasoning for wanting to take a fifth, if somewhat more official, test. 'I think you need to move past denial and work out what you're going to do. You need to talk to Jake. Have you got plans to see him before he goes to the country?'

Scarlett nodded. 'We're having breakfast in the morning.'

'Isn't he leaving tomorrow?'

She nodded again. 'He's driving down with a couple of other med students who are on different rotations. They're leaving at lunchtime.'

'You can't tell him minutes before he gets in the car,' Mel protested. 'Not when he's got a four-and-a-half-hour drive in front of him. That's not fair. Why are you waiting until the last minute?'

'I'm working all day today and he's working at The Coop tonight. Tomorrow is the only chance I've got.'

She was still getting used to the idea that she *might* be pregnant and she and Jake had both been flat out with other commitments over the past two days. She could think of half a dozen reasons why she hadn't said anything, half a dozen excuses for why she'd kept quiet, but she knew in reality she'd been stalling.

'You can't pretend this isn't happening.'

'Why not?' Might be pregnant was a whole different ballgame to definitely pregnant. Definitely pregnant meant having a baby and she wasn't sure she was ready to deal with that. Might be pregnant was working for her at the moment. She was hoping it was all a big mistake and that if she wished hard enough it would go away and she wouldn't have to say anything.

'Because eventually it's going to be obvious,' Mel said.

'If it's true,' Scarlett answered, but even as she uttered the words she knew that all the wishing in the world wasn't going to change the fact that she *was* pregnant. Four different tests had confirmed it, plus her period still hadn't come and the nausea hadn't gone away, neither had her aversion to coffee. Even her boobs were tender and she could swear they were already bigger. People *were* going to notice something, she couldn't keep denying it.

'Don't you think Jake deserves to hear it from you before other people find out?'

Mel was right. Jake would be in the country for the next month. She couldn't delay for much longer. 'Might be pregnant' was rapidly becoming 'time to face reality' and she couldn't risk him finding out some other way. She needed to tell him. She nodded.

'You'll have to go to The Coop tonight, then. I think you might need more than just an hour over breakfast to work this out. I'll come with you.'

'What for?'

'To make sure you don't chicken out.'

Scarlett had spent ages choosing an outfit. She knew she should be spending her time working out what she was going to say to Jake but sorting through her wardrobe was marginally less stressful and also managed to distract her from the thought of the dreaded conversation.

She didn't want to look like she was going into a business meeting, neither did she want to look like she was planning on clubbing until the wee hours of the morning, and eventually she settled on a wrap dress made of black jersey. Unfortunately the wrap style highlighted her breasts but she didn't have anything else suitable. She didn't think her boobs could get bigger than their normal DD but it seemed she was wrong and the black fabric wasn't enough to disguise her new dimensions. She'd decided to leave her hair loose, partly to try to soften her look and partly in an attempt to hide her boobs.

She'd also ditched the five-inch heels she'd borrowed

last time in favour of pointy-toed black patent leather boots with a two-inch heel. The boots were smart enough but far more comfortable and less stripper-like than the sandals and she thought far more suited to a pregnant woman, even if she did feel knocked up as opposed to pregnant.

But when Mel arrived to collect her Scarlett immediately felt mumsy by comparison, despite her kick-ass, pointy-toed boots. Mel was wearing a very short sequin tank dress with spaghetti straps, and she'd spiked up her short pixie hair and she looked edgy, like someone who belonged in the club. Scarlett's outfit could only be described as conservative next to Mel's.

Scarlett clutched her hands around her small handbag, holding it protectively in front of her as she looked around the club. Looking at the other patrons, she knew she'd be the least likely to be picked as the girl who'd have a one-night stand, let alone get pregnant, but that's was what she was. And even though their 'liaison' had turned into more than a one-night stand she was under no illusion that she and Jake had the sort of relationship that could handle having a baby together. Not yet. And probably not ever.

If ever there was a case of wrong place, wrong time, Scarlett thought this was it. She couldn't begin to imagine telling Jake her news in the club.

She scanned the room, aware that her heart was racing. She was terrified of telling Jake but Mel was right, he had a right to know. But she was still pinning her hopes on him not wanting the baby either. He was young and still studying. It was hardly good timing for him. He'd probably be scared too. Maybe they had other options.

But then she remembered how he interacted with his

niece and that he was contemplating doing paediatrics or obstetrics as his specialty, and she *knew* he would want the baby. Now she had to tell him about the baby *and* tell him *she* didn't want it.

Her eyes flicked over to the bar but she couldn't see Jake. Maybe he wasn't at work, maybe she'd got her wires crossed, maybe she could just go home. She was about to plead her case to Mel when the music started pumping and Mel nudged her in the ribs.

'There he is.'

Scarlett looked to the front of the room where three spotlights illuminated the catwalk. She could see Caesar and Rico and centre stage was Jake. All three of them were dressed alike in white T-shirts that hugged their chests and tight jeans that hugged their thighs, but Scarlett only had eyes for Jake.

The contrast between the three of them—Caesar bulky and dark, Rico lithe and serious and Jake ripped and cheeky—was interesting but Scarlett couldn't tear her eyes away from Jake. Their routine was well choreographed and well-rehearsed. Their movements were in perfect harmony as they played to the appreciative crowd but as Jake strutted down the catwalk she couldn't even pretend to be interested in anything or anyone but him.

As he gyrated his hips and winked at the women she hoped she was blending into the crowd. Jake in performance mode, even while fully clothed, was mesmerising and she wanted to enjoy the show anonymously.

The lyrics were familiar and she found herself moving to the beat of the song.

Jake's hands were at the neck of his T-shirt and she watched in fascination as he ripped his shirt in one smooth movement, tearing it down the middle to expose his chest.

Heat pooled low in her belly as he threw his shirt to one side before running his hands over his chest and along the ridge of his abdominals and down to his groin. She could feel the heat spreading from her stomach to her thighs and she was embarrassed by her lack of self-control.

Jake lifted his hands from his groin and linked his fingers behind his head, and his tattoo pulsed as his muscles flexed. His abdominal muscles rippled as he fell to his knees and women started shoving fistfuls of tipping dollars into his waistband as he winked and bestowed his cheeky grin on them. His star sign was most definitely a Leo.

Scarlett's mouth went dry as she watched the women go wild for Jake and suddenly, seeing him on stage performing for the adoring masses, wasn't so appealing. As he got to his feet he had his hands on his jeans and she knew what was coming next. She didn't need to see this. She didn't need to be reminded that she'd got herself knocked up by a stripper, even one as sexy and as intelligent as Jake. Could tonight get any worse?

CHAPTER NINE

SCARLETT WAS MORTIFIED. Her stomach heaved as she watched Jake, Caesar and Rico fall into position for the finale. She couldn't face what was coming next. She turned and fled to the ladies' room before Jake could rip his pants off and stand semi-naked in front of a room full of screaming women.

She was aware of Mel following her as she almost ran to the bathroom. Thank goodness the room was empty—everyone else was enjoying the show.

She got as far as the basins before she lost the contents of her stomach. Mel held her hair out of the way as she waited for her to finish vomiting.

'Wait here,' Mel told her when her stomach was finally empty, and Scarlett rinsed her mouth with tap water. 'I'll bring you a glass of water for a proper drink.'

When Mel came back Scarlett was sitting on a toilet seat with her head in her hands. 'I'm pregnant to a stripper,' she said, as Mel handed her the glass.

'It could be worse,' Mel replied.

'How could it possibly be worse?'

'It's not as if taking his clothes off is all he's good at. He's going to be a doctor, he's also a nice guy, cute, intelligent and, as an added bonus, all his bits appear to be in good working order.'

Scarlett groaned in response before rinsing her mouth again with the last of the water. 'I can't possibly talk to him now. I need to go home.'

'Give me a minute,' Mel said, as she took the glass and ducked out of the bathroom.

'I've left a message with Rooster,' she told Scarlett when she returned a few minutes later. 'I've asked Jake to call past your place when he knocks off. I've said it's urgent so now we can go home.'

It was late before Jake arrived but Mel had waited and she let him in before leaving.

He had stopped at the Blue and White Café. Scarlett could smell the yiros and recognised the wrapping.

'Are you hungry?' he asked as he bent to kiss her, before offering her one of the packets.

Scarlett held up one hand, refusing the wrap, and covered her mouth and nose with her other hand. The smell of the roast meat and garlic sauce made the bile rise in her throat.

'What's wrong? Are you sick?'

She shook her head. Her eyes were underlined with dark shadows and she knew she looked pale and tired, especially compared to Jake, who looked fantastically fit and healthy.

'I'm not sick,' she said, as she tugged on his hand, pulling him down to sit beside her. 'I'm pregnant.'

'Pregnant? Are you sure?'

She nodded. She knew she had to accept the facts. She couldn't deny it for ever.

'Shit. Pregnant? How many weeks are you?'

'Six, I think. It could only have happened that first time.'

'But we used protection.'

'Condoms are only ninety-eight per cent effective. Someone has to fall into the two per cent, and apparently it's us.'

'Have you had it confirmed?'

'There's no need. I've missed a period, I'm nauseous, I can't stand the smell of coffee or raw meat or apparently…' she waved her hand at his yiros '…garlic sauce. I've bought every home pregnancy test the pharmacy sells and they all came back positive. And my boobs are bigger.'

Jake smiled.

She stared at him as tears welled in her eyes. She felt like crying and he was smiling? What was the matter with him? She swallowed, fighting not to lose control. 'You think this is funny?'

'No, I know it's not,' he said, as he took one of her hands in his. Her hand felt cold against his warm palm. 'But I must say this isn't one of the first conversations I imagined us having when we moved on from our platonic status. I thought we might start with dinner and a movie. I was looking forward to getting to know you better, not choosing colours for a nursery.'

'Stop it.' Her voice caught as she fought back the tears. She couldn't believe he could see humour in their situation.

She shook her hand free from his hold but he wasn't going to let her go easily. He wrapped one arm around her shoulders and pulled her into him, resting her head against his chest as he kissed her forehead.

'Sorry. In our family we use humour when we're out of our depth. Somehow it helps make a crazy situation seem not so bad. In a family our size there's always someone with a bigger problem.'

'I'm not sure that it gets bigger than this.' Her voice was muffled against his body.

'Sure it does. People have been having children for thousands of years and plenty of them weren't planned. Other people cope. We'll manage too.'

'But I don't want children.'

He sat back, putting some distance between them so he could see her face. 'What do you mean, you don't want children?'

His tone suggested he'd never heard anything so ridiculous. Did he expect, just because she had a womb, that she had a desperate desire to reproduce? That one of her life's ambitions was to be a mother? He was about to learn a lot more about her than he'd bargained for.

'I didn't think you would want them either,' she said.

'Someday, in the future, definitely.'

'This isn't the future. This is happening now.'

He took hold of both her hands and fixed her in place with his green eyes. 'And so we will deal with it now. We can handle this.' His gaze was unwavering and she wanted to believe him. She almost did. Almost.

But she was scared.

'I'm not sure that I can.'

'Why not?'

'Because I don't want to. It's typical of my luck that the one time I do something out of character, something unplanned, I get into trouble. This wasn't ever something I wanted. This is why Richard and I broke up. He wanted children and I didn't. I wasn't prepared to give up my life to marry him and become a mother and I definitely don't want to be a single mother.'

'You don't have to go through this on your own, you know. It's my responsibility too.'

Scarlett shook her head. 'You can't promise that.'

'I can promise whatever I like.'

'There's nothing stopping you from walking away.'

'Nothing except my sense of duty and responsibility and family.'

'But you didn't ask for this any more than I did, and when it all gets too much? What then?'

He didn't answer immediately and Scarlett began to worry about what he was going to say. His answer surprised her.

'What is this really about?' he asked. 'I haven't said or done anything to make you think that when I give you my word I can't be trusted. What is bugging you?'

'Apart from the fact that I'm pregnant?' She managed a half smile, although she suspected it looked more like a grimace.

'Apart from that,' he agreed.

'I've seen how hard it is to raise a family, especially as a single mother. My mum had me when she was eighteen and I have never met my father. Mum struggled constantly to provide for my sisters and me and I have seen the sacrifices she had to make, and while I appreciate what she has done for me, for all of us, I don't want to be like her.'

'You've never met your father? But what about Ruby and Rose?'

She knew what he was asking. 'We're half-sisters. We all have different fathers. Our mother had three children by three different men. My father left before I was born. Ruby's father was a liar and adulterer. He had a whole other family in Melbourne that Mum didn't know about until she fell pregnant with Ruby. He was quite happy cheating on his wife but when Mum fell pregnant he got scared and went running back to Melbourne.'

'And what about Rose's dad?'

'He was lovely.'

'Was?'

Scarlett nodded. 'He married Mum when I was eight. That was the happiest time for all of us. We still didn't have much money but we were a family. But he died when I was sixteen.'

'What happened?'

'He was much older than Mum and he died suddenly of a heart attack. Mum has been on her own ever since.'

'Does your father know about you?'

Scarlett nodded. 'He knew Mum was pregnant. Mum told him. That's only right, isn't it? The father should know?' she asked, seeking confirmation from him.

'Most definitely. Do you know where your father is?'

She shook her head. 'No.'

'Have you tried to track him down?'

'I figure he doesn't want to see me. He could have looked for me. He could have looked for my mother. He knew where to start at least. But this isn't about my father. This is about me. I've watched my mother struggle as a single mum. I've seen what she gave up to raise me and my sisters. I've lived it and I don't want to battle for the rest of my life. I know what it's like to be poor, to wear second-hand clothes, to share a bed with my siblings, to say no to birthday parties because we couldn't afford to buy a present, and I can't consider putting my career on hold to raise a child. I've worked hard to make something of my life and I'm not done yet. I don't want to give it up now.'

'Why would you have to give it up?' he asked. 'You don't need to worry. You didn't get into this situation on your own. It's my responsibility too and I won't let you down. I know you're scared but I'm not going to abandon you. We are in this together.'

He was handling the news far better than she'd expected, far better than she was, but she wasn't sure if she could believe him.

'How can you be so sure? This has come completely out of the blue. We might end up hating each other,' she said, but she was thinking, *You'll end up leaving me.*

'Whatever happens, it will still be my child.'

'Are you saying you really *want* to be a father now?' She had assumed he wouldn't want a baby either at this point in his life.

'I'm saying I don't like the alternatives and you can trust me to do the right thing.'

Trusting men to keep their word wasn't something she was very good at, particularly when they were promising to stay. She appreciated the sentiment but she wasn't convinced she believed it and she was too tired to give it the consideration she needed to. She couldn't think about it any more tonight. The sun would be up in a few hours and she needed some sleep and so did he.

'I need some time to think about this.'

He didn't push her. He just nodded. 'Do you want me to delay the drive tomorrow? I can leave later.'

'No. We need more than a couple of hours to think this over.'

'All right. But don't make any big decisions without talking to me first, okay?'

'Okay.'

Jake kissed her gently on the lips, his touch light and soft and warm. Scarlett closed her eyes, savouring his taste. He rested his hand on her stomach, deliberately or not, she wasn't sure, but her belly fluttered under his fingers. She knew it was just her normal reaction to his touch but part of her imagined it was the fluttering of a tiny baby. 'Look after yourself. I'll talk to you soon,' he said. And then he was gone and she was alone.

She knew it wasn't his fault, she knew he had to go, but she couldn't help but feel he was already leaving her.

He was almost home. It had been a long first week on his country placement. The hours in Obstetrics were always erratic and often long but it was the additional stress of Scarlett's unexpected pregnancy that had pushed the limits of his endurance. He knew Scarlett was worried about him managing the long drive at the end of a working week and even though he'd told her he was fine, that he was used to long hours, he felt tired and he knew apprehension was contributing to his fatigue.

When he had spoken to Scarlett during the week he'd heard the consternation in her voice and he knew she was still undecided about the pregnancy. He couldn't admit to himself that she was undecided about the baby. Their baby, his baby. His child.

Even though the timing wasn't perfect he was excited about the news, but Scarlett's hesitancy was certainly spoiling the moment. He could understand how their very different upbringings were causing conflicting emotions for them both but he hadn't expected her to be so set against the pregnancy. He'd meant it when he'd said he'd be there for her. He would support her in any way she wanted, but his child came first and he knew he would fight for his unborn child with every cell in his body until he took his last breath.

He had spent almost every spare minute of the past week looking at his options and getting the finer details from his brother-in-law, Ted, who was a family lawyer.

But what Ted had told him hadn't eased his mind or solved his dilemma.

According to Ted, and in Australian law, a father had no rights over an unborn child. If Scarlett didn't want this baby apparently there wasn't much he could do about it, but he refused to accept that as final.

He drummed his fingers on the steering-wheel as he waited for the traffic lights at the bottom of the freeway to turn green. Fifteen more minutes and he hoped he'd start to get some answers.

It didn't go quite as he planned. With Scarlett, nothing ever went as planned.

He had imagined presenting a reasonable, logical and rational argument to convince Scarlett to have their baby, but all sensible thought evaporated as soon as he saw her.

She greeted him at the door wearing a silk robe, which was loosely tied at her waist, and he knew that with one tug the robe would fall away and that underneath she'd be naked.

He managed to resist until she had closed the front door and then he reached for her. His mouth covered hers as his fingers undid her robe. Scarlett moaned as his fingers brushed her bare skin as he pushed the robe from her shoulders. It fell to the floor with a soft rustle as he scooped her up and carried her into her bedroom, and all arguments were forgotten as they made up for the week apart.

The good mood lasted until they were both spent and satisfied. Until he had showered and they were sitting in the kitchen, sharing a midnight supper of scrambled eggs.

'I've been thinking about our situation. I think we should get married,' he said.

'What on earth for?'

'I know you're scared. I thought if we were married it would give you security. I want to raise our baby together, as a family.' Jake had thought he had worked out where her reluctance was coming from. She wanted financial security but he suspected she also wanted emotional security, and he was prepared to offer her that.

'We both know that being married is no guarantee that a relationship will last,' she argued. 'It's no guarantee of anything and it's not the 1960s. I don't want to get married because I'm pregnant. I don't even want to be pregnant.'

Had he misread her story so badly? He had tried to see things from her perspective but had he still got it completely wrong?'

'This could be the adventure you're supposed to have.'

'This is not my idea of an adventure.'

She obviously hadn't changed her mind over the past week. He was prepared to do the right thing, he was prepared to support her in any way she wanted, but his child had to be his priority. He moved to Plan B.

'Scarlett, I want this baby. I want our baby. I know you're worried about doing this on your own but I want to be part of this. If I have to I will raise our baby alone but I need one thing from you, I need you to stay pregnant. I'm begging you, please, don't do anything rash.'

'You work in a strip club. How on earth are you going to have time to raise a baby?'

'You and I both know I won't be working there for ever. At the end of the year I'll be a doctor. I'll be an intern. I won't be working in the bar and I will have a decent income.'

'And then you want to specialise. You'll be study-

ing for years to come. You can't take time off to care
for a baby and neither can I. The future doesn't take
care of itself.'

'I have money saved, I own my apartment, I can provide for my child.'

'I appreciate you want to do this but in my experience men don't stick around. What happens when you're
working eighty-hour weeks as an intern? What happens
when you want to travel back to Asia? What happens
when you start to feel trapped? I'll end up alone with
the baby, a single mother.'

'Have I told you about the programme at Blue Lake
Hospital?' he asked. 'Annie Simpson, the obstetrician
who is supervising me, runs a programme for teenage
mothers in conjunction with the high school to help the
girls to finish school and keep their babies. If teenagers
can do it, you can too.'

'This isn't part of my plan.'

'We can make a new plan. We can work this out. Together. You're strong and smart and you're not going to
have to do this alone.'

'I'm not strong enough. I'm not like my mother.'

'You don't have to be. I will be there for you.' But
it was obvious to him now that Scarlett didn't think
he would be enough. 'What has your mum said?' he
asked. Maybe someone else's opinion would help her
to see sense.

Scarlett didn't reply, she just shook her head.

'Have you told your mum about the baby? Have you
told Ruby?'

'No. I don't want to tell anyone. I don't want it to
be real.'

'Why haven't you said anything?'

'I'm worried that Mum will be disappointed in me.'

'Your mother raised three daughters on her own. If anyone will understand, she will.'

'I don't want to repeat her mistakes.'

'Has she ever told you that you were a mistake?'

'I know I was.'

'You were unplanned but she chose to have you. Do you think she'd want you to make a different choice? You have a career, you have my support. You're in a much better position than she was. Has she ever complained about the sacrifices she made? Has she ever told you she didn't want you?'

'No.'

'I think you should talk to her. You can't make decisions based on your mother's experiences. Especially if you don't really know what her experience was. You are in a very different position. Can I ask you, please, before you make a decision, will you do me a favour and talk to your mum?'

It took all weekend but Jake finally thought he'd managed to convince Scarlett to at least talk to her mother. He knew that conversation could go one of two ways but he hoped it would persuade her to keep the baby. He was prepared to raise a child, his child, alone if he had to. He had no doubt he could but he'd prefer to do it with Scarlett. He knew they could do it together, he just had to convince her to trust him and that was the difficult part. He wasn't sure how he was going to achieve that but he wasn't going to give up yet.

CHAPTER TEN

SCARLETT SAT ON the couch opposite her mother. Her heart was racing and her hands were shaking so badly she had to lace her fingers together and hold her hands in her lap to disguise the tremor. She was more nervous now than she'd been when she'd told Jake the news. She was only here because Jake had asked her to let her mother know. He had been so supportive she felt she owed him this at least.

Jake made her feel good about herself but she wasn't feeling so good at the moment. She felt like she was letting him down. She wasn't being the person she knew he wanted her to be. She wasn't sure if she *could* be that person. Was he asking too much or was she being unfair?

She sat quietly, waiting while her mother poured their tea. Her mother always insisted on making tea properly, in a warmed teapot and using fine bone-china cups. Scarlett normally found the routine soothing and had asked for tea specifically for that purpose, but today nothing was comforting.

'What's the matter, darling?' Lucy asked, as she passed Scarlett her cup and saucer. 'Nothing's so terrible that you can't tell me about it.'

'How do you know something's wrong?'

'I'm your mother, I can tell when something is troubling you.'

She took a deep breath. 'I'm pregnant.'

'Oh, thank God.' Lucy moved seats, coming to sit beside Scarlett as she hugged her. 'I'm so pleased.'

'You are?'

'Yes. You look exhausted and you look like you've lost weight. I thought you were going to tell me you were sick. But pregnant! That's exciting.'

Scarlett hadn't expected that. 'Is it? I thought you'd think I was crazy.'

'Why?'

Scarlett shrugged. 'Another Anderson female getting knocked up while single.'

'It's hardly the worst thing that can happen,' Lucy replied matter-of-factly, 'but you don't sound thrilled with your news. Are you having doubts?'

Scarlett nodded. 'I don't want to be pregnant. It's really not part of my plan, short term or long term. I broke up with Richard because he wanted kids. His heart attack was the catalyst for his change of mind but it scared me. I was terrified I'd end up alone, raising his family, and that was not what I wanted for my future.'

'Is Richard the father?'

Scarlett shook her head. 'No. It's more complicated than that.'

'What are you going to do?'

'I don't know yet. Do you ever think of how different your life would have been if you hadn't fallen pregnant with me? Did you ever think of not having me?'

'No.' Lucy shook her head. 'Not once. My life would certainly have been different but it couldn't have been any better. I wouldn't want to change a thing.'

'But I saw how hard your life was. I've lived through the struggle.'

'I'm not pretending that being a single mother is easy but you're in a much better position than I was. You're twelve years older than I was when I fell pregnant, that puts a completely different spin on things, and you have a career. A very good career.'

'I always thought Ruby would be the one to make a mistake. I would have placed money on Ruby being in this situation before me.'

Lucy smiled but refrained from commenting. She never compared her girls. 'Don't think of your pregnancy as a mistake,' she said. 'A baby is a gift. I know you want a different life to the one I've had. I want that for you too. But if I had to choose between having you girls or having an easy life I would do it all again, exactly the same. I love you more than anything in the world.

'I know it hasn't always been easy but the best things in life are often the things worth fighting for. Not everything in life works out exactly how you'd like it to or planned for. But some of life's surprises can be the best things that ever happen to you. Sometimes they can take you on an adventure you never expected.'

Scarlett wondered why everyone kept talking about adventure. What were they seeing that she wasn't?

'I don't know if I have the courage to be a single mother.'

'You'll find the strength if you need to. Trust me, once this baby is born there is nothing you won't do for him or her. I know you've worked hard at your studies but that just means that you will be financially secure. You can raise a baby. You'll be surprised at how your priorities will change. I know you—once you hold that baby in your arms you will do anything to protect him or her. A mother's love is like no other. You'll wonder how you ever doubted yourself.'

Lucy sipped her tea before asking, 'But why are you assuming you'll be a single mother? What about the baby's father? Does he know? How does he feel?'

'He wants the baby. He wants to be involved.' Scarlett didn't tell her mother that Jake had offered to raise the baby on his own if need be. She wasn't sure how she felt about that yet.

'Is it serious between you?'

'I don't know. I thought it could be but it's only early days. I was looking forward to seeing how things developed between us but being pregnant is a complicating factor I wasn't expecting and I'm not sure now if we've missed our opportunity. If I have the baby nothing will be the same again but if I choose *not* to have the baby that will change everything anyway.'

'Are you considering a termination?'

'I don't think I'm brave enough to go through with it. And Jake wants the baby. Knowing that, I don't think I could do it. It doesn't seem right. None of this seems right.'

'I've always been a big believer in the saying that things happen for a reason. Do you love Jake?'

'I don't know that either. When I'm with him everything feels right, as if my world is in balance. I'm not aware of anything else when he's beside me. He calms me and excites me at the same time. I feel alive. I feel happy. I feel like I'm the person I'm supposed to be.'

'That's how I felt about your father.'

'Really?'

Lucy nodded. 'I loved your father. We might have

been young but nothing was as important to me as he was until you came along.'

'What happened to you both? Why wasn't he around?'

'I thought he would be. I thought we were going to raise you together but his family had other plans. They didn't want him throwing his future away by becoming a teenage father. His family moved interstate, they deliberately took him away and they paid for me to terminate the pregnancy.'

'You were going to have a termination?' Scarlett's stomach dropped. She'd had no idea her mother had considered not having her. She was horrified to think she might not have existed and she knew then that as much as she wished not to be pregnant, there had never really been any question that she wouldn't keep the baby.

'Obviously I couldn't do it. I had to keep you.'

Scarlett had always believed her father knew about her. What if that wasn't the case? What if he thought the pregnancy had been terminated? 'Does my father know you kept me? Did you tell him?'

'Yes, of course. Your grandparents made sure of it. But I never heard anything from him.'

'And you never tried to find him?'

'No.' Lucy shook her head. 'I always hoped he'd come looking for us but he never did. He broke my heart and I was angry and afraid, but I recovered once I had you. I had to. I poured all that love into you and tried not to think about your father.'

'Are you sorry about how things worked out?'

'I have no regrets. I've been lucky in so many ways. I got something wonderful from our relationship. I got you. Love is a gamble. A risk. You can't make someone love you but you have to be prepared to take the chance that they will. But the one thing you don't have to gamble on is the love you will feel for a child of your own.'

Her mother's words resonated with her. It was time to stop wishing for a father she'd never known, for a father who had never wanted to know her. She couldn't change the past and she'd wasted many years wishing for something she wasn't going to get. He didn't deserve her time. She didn't owe him anything. She owed her mother and now she owed it to her unborn child to look after him or her. She had other priorities. She put her hand over her stomach. She could feel a mother's love already.

She saw her mother notice her gesture. 'Sometimes you have to trust in yourself and sometimes you have to learn to trust other people,' Lucy told her. 'You have one life to live and this is it. Nothing matters except this baby. You'll realise that soon enough. You'll work out what the right thing is to do.'

Scarlett had the opportunity to give her own child the very thing she herself had wanted. Her own child had a father who wanted her and she couldn't deny her child that right. She had to do her best for her own baby and that included giving it a chance to know Jake.

Scarlett slowed her car as she approached the outskirts of Penola. She was almost there. Another forty minutes and she would be with Jake.

The countryside was getting prettier. This was wine country, the famous Coonawarra district, and rows of grapevines ran in perfectly straight lines out into the distance on both sides of the road, their symmetry only broken by the occasional enormous old gum tree or small creek or picturesque stone building. Many of the numerous wineries had modern cellar door and visitor facilities but the town itself looked as though it hadn't changed for a hundred years. She stopped to buy a cold drink and stretch her legs but didn't want to waste precious minutes dawdling here when she could be on her way to Jake.

She got back on the road and her mind wandered as she drove out of town. She wondered if they'd have a chance over the weekend to come back here for a meal as most of the wineries appeared to have a restaurant, or maybe they could just browse in some of the shops.

The road veered to the right around a blind corner and Scarlett eased her foot off the accelerator, her unfamiliarity with the highway making her cautious.

She rounded the corner and was shocked to find herself face to face with a wine tanker that was halfway across the road and taking up most of her lane. Desperate to get out of its way, she yanked on the steering-wheel and was relieved when the truck missed the side of her car by inches. But her relief was short-lived.

Her evasive action had forced her partially off the road and before she could correct her drift her car was hit by the airstream from the moving truck and forced further sideways. She felt herself losing control of the car as her outside tyres lost traction on the loose stones at the roadside. Her speed and momentum took over and carried her car completely off the road.

The car was skidding across the dirt but somehow she managed to resist the temptation to hit the brakes and instead remembered what Sean had taught her on the skid pan. *Steer into the skid.*

It had seemed strange then and it seemed even stranger now, but she tried to do what she'd been taught. She turned the car into the skid.

But she was still sliding. She hoped the car wasn't going to roll.

She waited, fighting to get the wheels aligned. Her knuckles were white as she gripped the steering-wheel and waited for the car to straighten. She knew she was supposed to wait until the moment the wheels were aligned again before she accelerated out of the skid. Were they aligned yet? She didn't know.

She was aware of a scraping sound and an occasional thwack of branches as the car careered through the scrubby bush. This was a totally different experience to the skid pan. On the skid pan there'd been no outside interference, nothing to interrupt her concentration and nothing that had really been a threat to her safety. Looming in the passenger window was a tree, more than one, actually. There certainly hadn't been any trees in the middle of the skid pan.

She had no clue what to do now. If she did nothing, she was going to hit a tree.

Were her wheels aligned yet? She had no idea.

Her survival instinct took over. She took a chance and touched her foot to the accelerator pedal, hoping her wheels were aligned, hoping and praying she could now drive out of the skid. The car surged forward as she depressed the pedal but she didn't have full control and she felt the back of the car slide sideways again.

The car was fighting her. There was nothing she could do.

She heard the crunch of metal, a thud and her world went dark.

'Jake, we've got a consult in Emergency. MVA with a pregnant woman.'

Jake's eyes flicked to the clock on the wall. He hadn't

heard from Scarlett yet, he'd expected her in the last half hour. His gut contracted so violently he thought he was going to throw up. He felt the blood rush from his head and he gripped the counter at the nurses' station as he tried to steady himself.

'Jake?' He felt Annie's hand on his shoulder. 'Are you okay?' Her words were jumbled, the sound of the blood rushing from his head loud enough to partially drown out her voice.

'Scarlett.' His voice caught in his throat and sounded husky and hoarse. 'Did they give you a name?'

'No.' Annie shook her head. 'But whoever it is, she's alive. Let's get down there and we'll find out.'

There was an ambulance in the bay. The doors were open and the paramedics were unloading a stretcher. Jake caught a glimpse of raven hair and he took off, sprinting past Thang, the doctor on duty.

'Jake! What are you doing?'

'That's my—' What was she? Girlfriend, partner, mother of my child? How did he describe her?

She was his everything.

He loved every contrary and complex thing about her and he wasn't going to let anything bad happen to her. He'd promised to take care of her and that started now.

Seeing her lying pale and still on the stretcher with her dark hair spread around her she looked like Sleeping Beauty, except for the bloody gash at her temple. His heart beat a loud and angry tattoo in his chest. She was injured. But how badly?

He was by her side and his hand sought hers. 'Scarlett?'

Her eyelids flickered open and he could see her searching for him. Her eyes darted from side to side. Her neck was immobilised in a cervical collar and she couldn't turn her head. He hoped the collar was only a precaution. 'Jake?' He leant over the stretcher as the paramedics wheeled her inside.

'I'm here.' He squeezed her fingers gently and relief flooded through him as he felt her squeeze his fingers in return.

'The baby?'

'Let's get you into an exam room. Everything will be okay.' He hoped he was right.

He ran his eyes over her as they rushed her inside the hospital. She was covered with a dusting of fine white powder from the airbag but apart from the gash at her temple he couldn't see any other external signs of injury.

She was taken straight into a treatment room. Jake followed but Thang stopped him just inside. 'We need to do a general exam,' he told him, and Jake knew Thang meant him to wait outside.

'I'm fine. I want you to check the baby first.' Scarlett lifted one hand from the stretcher, holding it up to stop Thang. Jake saw her wince with the movement but she didn't back down. 'I'm a doctor too, I know I don't have any life-threatening injuries.' She looked at Jake, her dark eyes pleading with him. 'Don't you think I'd tell you if there was anything serious, anything that could harm the baby?'

A week ago he wasn't sure if he could have given her the answer she wanted but looking at her now he knew her concern for their child was genuine. Something had happened in the last week that had made her certain about this baby. Something had made her become the mother he knew she could be.

His heart swelled with love. For Scarlett and their baby. He smiled and nodded. 'Scarlett's right,' he told Thang. 'Let's check the baby first.'

'Are you really okay?' he asked once Thang had agreed with the order of examination and Scarlett had been transferred from the stretcher to a bed.

Scarlett nodded. 'I'm fine, thanks to you.'

'Me?'

'I think if you hadn't taken me on that skid-pan exercise, things might have been a lot worse. That might have saved my life but I'm still worried the baby—'

'All right, that's my cue,' Annie interrupted. 'I'm Annie Simpson, the ob-gyn. Let's have a look at this baby, shall we? How many weeks are you?'

'I think maybe eight.'

'Have you had any prenatal appointments?' Annie asked as she took control of the situation.

'No.'

'Any unusual symptoms—spotting, cramping, pain?'

'Now or before?'

'Before today.'

'Just morning sickness but I've got pain here now.' She lifted her shirt and ran her hand lightly across her lower abdomen.

The nurse wrapped a blood-pressure cuff around Scarlett's arm and slipped an oxygen monitor onto her finger, while Annie flicked the ultrasound monitor on and squeezed gel onto the transducer head of the ultrasound. 'If you're eight-weeks gestation, an abdominal ultrasound will tell us what we need to know. This gel will be a little cold, I haven't had time to warm it up,' Annie said, as she squeezed a little onto Scarlett's stomach.

Jake pulled a chair beside the bed and held Scarlett's hand. Annie adjusted the angle of the monitor so everyone could see and then began to sweep the ultrasound head across Scarlett's belly. A black-and-white image appeared on the screen. They all knew what they were looking for.

A black pocket appeared on the screen. Scarlett's uterus. Inside the pocket was a tiny figure, shaped like a jelly baby.

'Oh.' Scarlett lifted her hand and reached for the screen, almost as though she wanted to hold the baby.

Annie moved the ultrasound head slowly. 'There's a good strong heartbeat.' They could see a tiny flicker of a pulse on the screen. 'That's a good sign.'

A tear rolled down Scarlett's cheek. Jake leant over and gently kissed it away. 'It's all fine,' he told her. 'We're all going to be fine.'

Annie pushed a few buttons and took some measurements. 'Your baby seems perfectly okay and I'd say you're pretty spot on with your dates. It all looks about right for eight weeks. You can see the limb buds, the arms and legs just here.' She pushed another button and printed a picture. She handed it to Scarlett. 'Congratulations, the first picture for your album.'

'Can you believe it?' Scarlett said, as they stared at the picture. 'It's really happening.'

'I wish I could give you some time together but Thang will want to come in and examine Scarlett now,' Annie told them.

Jake nodded. He intended to stay with Scarlett but Thang banned him from the exam room.

'I should be in there with her,' he said to Annie, as he paced nervously outside.

'Let Thang do his job,' Annie told him. 'He doesn't need you hovering over his shoulder. The baby is fine and Scarlett seems okay too. You can relax.'

But he couldn't relax. Not until he knew the state of affairs.

Thang reappeared from the exam room. He pulled off his gloves as he delivered a reassuring summary. 'Soft-tissue injuries in the main. Whiplash, mild concussion, some bruising from the seat belt and possibly a cracked rib, but overall it seems as though she was very lucky. No apparent liver, kidney or spleen injuries. She's refusing any pain relief so she really just needs rest. You can go back in now.'

'Can I take her home?' Jake looked at both Annie and Thang.

Thang nodded while Annie replied, 'Ordinarily I'd keep her in for observation—'

'I promise not to let her out of my sight.'

'All right. I'll arrange for someone to collect her things from her car. It'll be towed into town, but she'll need a few things in the meantime, some clothes and toiletries and the like. Why don't you organise that and then you can come back and pick her up?'

Jake hadn't considered the practicalities. All he wanted was to get Scarlett out of here and into the five-star accommodation he'd booked for them for the weekend. It had been a far better option than taking her to the hospital accommodation he was sharing with two other med students but Annie's suggestion made sense and the sooner he followed her instructions the sooner he'd have Scarlett to himself.

'Are you in pain?' Jake asked her.

'No. Well, yes, but I'm okay.' Talking was painful. *Breathing* was painful but Scarlett wasn't going to complain. She was lucky to still be doing those things.

She lay in the warm bath that Jake had drawn for her and she felt good, battered and bruised but good. The accommodation was gorgeous. The marble bathroom was huge and luxurious and their room had a soft king-sized bed, a log fire and French doors that opened onto a private patio area overlooking the expansive grounds of the rural resort. It was a room made for champagne and romance but she'd have to make do with the romance. Surrounded by bubbles of a different kind, cocooned in the warm water and drinking a hot chocolate while candles flickered on the basin edge, she felt quite decadent. 'I can put up with some discomfort now that I know the baby is okay.'

'You sound far more positive than you did a week ago. I was worried you weren't going to have the baby. What's changed?'

Jake was sitting at the end of the bath. He was wearing jeans but his chest and feet were bare. This was one of her favourite Jakes. She ran her eyes over his naked torso. 'Why don't you join me in here and I'll tell you.'

'I don't think there's room for me.'

'I'll make room.' She smiled and slid forward in the bath. She watched as Jake stood and unbuttoned his jeans, dropping them to the floor along with his underwear. Just a glimpse of him naked was enough to elevate her pulse.

He slipped into the bath behind her, pulling her back to nestle between his thighs. Scarlett could feel his arousal and she was tempted to take advantage of it but she knew she needed to tell him what she was thinking, and if she didn't take the opportunity now who knew when she'd have another one?

'You were right,' she said, as he wrapped his arms around her. 'I had a few things to sort out but Mum and I had a big talk, like you asked, and she made me realise some things about myself and my life.

'Growing up, I always wished I had a father. I wanted

to be like the other girls at school. I used to make up stories about why my dad wasn't around. I think my favourite was when I told everyone he was a spy, and when I was older and Mum married Rose's dad I claimed him as my own and said he'd just returned from a secret mission. Rose's dad was lovely and he treated me like I was his own daughter. I don't think I would have been any happier with my own father, but part of me always felt as though something was missing.

'Mum has only just told me that my father's family wanted her to terminate the pregnancy, terminate me, which was something I never knew. When Mum told me I realised I could never do that and was never thinking that way. I was just wishing I wasn't pregnant, which isn't the same thing as not wanting the baby. Accepting I was pregnant was my major hurdle.

'I spent years wishing I had a father when I should have been grateful that I had a mother who loved me and chose to keep me. Knowing how much easier things would have been for her if she had terminated the pregnancy made me realise that I am in the same situation and I am choosing to make the same decision she did. All I wanted was a father of my own and I want to be able to give my own child the chance I never had. It wouldn't be fair of me to take that away from the baby or from you.

'But I should warn you. Trust is difficult for me. Because Mum's relationships didn't last I expected the same from mine, and I know I often don't give anyone a chance. I expect them to leave. My mother and my sisters have been my roots. They keep me anchored to the ground and I've always worried that if I give myself to someone else they might rip me from the roots and then discard me. I felt I might disintegrate and disappear like the seeds of a dandelion blown by the wind. But the past is just that, and it's Mum's past, not mine. I need to take a chance.'

Jake kissed the side of her neck, just at the point where it joined her shoulder. 'I will be your shelter,' he said. 'I will protect you and any little seeds that fall from you. Those seeds are the beginnings of a new family, our family, and I will protect you all and be there always. I promise you. Will you do this with me?'

Scarlett nodded. 'I want to see whether we can build a relationship. I was worried that this pregnancy had ruined any chance we had but then I realised it was me who was jeopardising that. If you're prepared to trust in us then so am I.'

'Do you want to look for your father?'

'No. I've thought about this a lot this week. Why I've never gone looking for him myself when I've had years when I could have searched for him. But I know it was because I was scared to. I didn't want him to reject me. I don't know if I never want to find him but that is a question for another day.

'What I do know is that I want my own child to know you. That's what's important now. I need to build my own future, our future, and to do that I need to trust in you and believe that we can make this work or at least be prepared to give it our best shot. I can't continue to make assumptions about my life based on the past. I need to look to the future and I want you to be a part of that. Starting now.

'I am going to focus on you, me and our baby. On seeing if we have a relationship that can work. You were right. Things haven't worked out exactly as I planned but they may turn out to be better. This will be the biggest adventure of my life and if you are prepared to go on it with me I think I might just survive.'

They had made love in the enormous bed. Scarlett had insisted she was fine and he'd been unable to resist, although they had taken it slowly, carefully and tenderly. She was propped up in bed, her dark eyes enormous in her pale face, but despite her pallor he thought she'd never looked more beautiful.

He had drawn the curtains and lit the gas log fire and the room was illuminated only by the soft light of the flames. Now was the perfect time to give Scarlett his present.

He reached into the drawer of the bedside table where he had hidden the package earlier. 'I have something for you,' he said, as he handed her a gift bag.

Scarlett peeked inside and pulled out a wooden matryoshka doll.

'She's beautiful. What is she for?'

'For you. She reminds me of you.'

Scarlett frowned. 'She does?'

'Yes. Remember when I described you as the parcel in the pass-the-parcel game?'

Scarlett laughed. 'Yes. Not the most flattering description.'

'I agree, and I've decided that you're still layered but perhaps you're more like one of these dolls. Complex but within every layer is something else equally as interesting and equally as valuable.'

'Where on earth did you find her?' Scarlett asked. 'She even looks a bit like me,' she said, as she studied her closely. The first doll was a woman with her dark hair pulled into a bun and with an intricately detailed face, dark eyes and full lips, dressed in a white doctor's coat with a stethoscope around her neck.

'I had her made for you. There's a local artist who makes these to order. This is you in all your different complexities. The doctor,' he said as Scarlett separated the first doll to reveal one wearing a replica of the paisley dress she'd worn to Candice's wedding. 'The party you.' Next was Scarlett the sister. The artist had painted tiny images of Ruby and Rose on either side of her, and then there was Scarlett dressed in white, a lace veil covering her dark hair.

'Is this a wedding dress?'

Jake nodded as Scarlett shook the doll. Something rattled inside.

She looked at him, her dark eyes wide. 'I'm not ready for marriage. It's not a ring, is it?'

'It's okay, open it.' He smiled.

Inside was another doll. Still Scarlett but this time dressed in a simple pale pink shirt. It still rattled.

'There's one more,' Jake said.

Nestled inside was a tiny doll.

Scarlett lifted it out. It was a dark-eyed baby wrapped in a swaddling cloth.

Jake picked up the final empty doll and pushed the two halves back together before cupping it in his hand. 'This doll is you, the mother, and this…' he rolled his finger over the baby '…is our baby. There's no ring. Not yet. I am going to marry you but only when you are ready. I believe we were meant to meet at this point in our lives. This baby is meant to be ours and we are meant to be together. Married or not, we're ready for this.' He kissed her gently before asking. 'Do you remember why I got my tattoo?'

Scarlett nodded. 'To remind you to always come home.'

'You and our baby are my home now. I will always be there for you. For both of you. I want to marry you because I love you.' He rested his hand over her belly. 'I love you both. Just tell me when you are ready.'

Scarlett closed her palm around the baby doll, cradling it in her hand. She slid her hand under Jake's and wrapped his fingers around hers, holding them together. 'I'm not ready yet but I know this is where I'm supposed to be. With you. I love you too.'

EPILOGUE

'CAN YOU BELIEVE it? In one week you'll be Mrs Chamberlain.'

Scarlett was in the kitchen, chopping vegetables for a salad, when Jake came up behind her and wrapped his arms around her swollen belly as he kissed her neck. It was ten days until Christmas and the temperature had been climbing steadily for weeks. Scarlett was feeling huge and uncomfortably pregnant but the touch of Jake's hand was enough to make her forget her discomfort.

'I can't wait to see you walk down the aisle.'

'Don't you mean waddle?' she said, as she turned her head and smiled at her fiancé.

'No. You look beautiful. This last trimester suits you,' he said, as he slipped his hand inside her loose camisole and cupped her breast.

Scarlett moaned as his fingers teased her nipple, sending shivers of longing through her. She didn't know about this last trimester suiting her but it had certainly fired up her libido. It seemed all Jake had to do was look at her and she felt like ripping all his clothes off. Hers too.

'I have something to show you,' Jake said. 'An early wedding present.'

'Ooh, what is it? You know I love presents.'

In reply Jake pulled his T-shirt over his head and the sight of his naked torso almost made Scarlett forget about the present. He was too gorgeous for words. He had finished his undergraduate medical degree and left his job at The Coop in order to spend more time with her before he started his internship, but he had kept up his exercise routine and still looked fabulous.

Scarlett ran her eyes over his body in appreciation and it was then she noticed a sterile dressing on his left upper arm.

Concern flooded through her. 'What happened to you?' she asked, reaching out one hand towards his arm.

Jake's fingers teased the edge of the dressing, pulling it from his skin where it had covered his tattoo.

'I got a new tattoo,' he told her.

He lifted his arm and Scarlett could see two new stars inked on his arm at a forty-five-degree angle to the Southern Cross.

'What are they?'

'Alpha and Beta Centauri, the Pointer Stars.' He pointed to the first star, furthest from the Southern Cross. 'This one is you and this one,' he said, pointing to the second new star, 'is our baby. The two of you will always guide me home. Every time you see these stars I want you to remember that you can depend on me. I love you and I can't wait to spend the rest of my life taking care of you.'

Scarlett linked her arms around his neck. 'I do know that. It's one of the reasons I agreed to marry you.'

'What were the others?'

'You make me feel safe, adored and happy. I love you and if we didn't have to wait for all our siblings to get home I'd marry you tomorrow.'

'Haven't you learnt by now that I'm a patient man?'

'I have learnt that. It's another reason why I agreed to marry you. You waited so long for me to give you an answer I thought you deserved it to be yes.

'Five months was about my limit,' he teased. 'Any other reasons spring to mind?'

'Yes. I can't resist your tattoos.'

'You like these.' Jake grinned at her and flexed his biceps.

'I do.' She ran her fingers lightly up his arm and reached behind his head. She pulled his forward and kissed him hard on the mouth. 'Shall I show you just how much?' she whispered. She dropped her hands to the waistband of his shorts and discovered his reaction was as intense as hers. 'It looks like you're not that patient after all.' She laughed.

'There is only so much waiting I can do in one lifetime,' he said, as Scarlett divested him of the rest of his clothes. 'And it seems I've just run out of patience,' he added, as he scooped her into his arms and carried her off to bed.

* * * * *

ROMANCE

A Virgin for His Prize	Lucy Monroe
The Valquez Seduction	Melanie Milburne
Protecting the Desert Princess	Carol Marinelli
One Night with Morelli	Kim Lawrence
To Defy a Sheikh	Maisey Yates
The Russian's Acquisition	Dani Collins
The True King of Dahaar	Tara Pammi
Rebel's Bargain	Annie West
The Million-Dollar Question	Kimberly Lang
Enemies with Benefits	Louisa George
Man vs. Socialite	Charlotte Phillips
Fired by Her Fling	Christy McKellen
The Twelve Dates of Christmas	Susan Meier
At the Chateau for Christmas	Rebecca Winters
A Very Special Holiday Gift	Barbara Hannay
A New Year Marriage Proposal	Kate Hardy
A Little Christmas Magic	Alison Roberts
Christmas with the Maverick Millionaire	Scarlet Wilson

MEDICAL

Playing the Playboy's Sweetheart	Carol Marinelli
Unwrapping Her Italian Doc	Carol Marinelli
A Doctor by Day...	Emily Forbes
Tamed by the Renegade	Emily Forbes

Mills & Boon® Large Print

November 2014

ROMANCE

Christakis's Rebellious Wife	Lynne Graham
At No Man's Command	Melanie Milburne
Carrying the Sheikh's Heir	Lynn Raye Harris
Bound by the Italian's Contract	Janette Kenny
Dante's Unexpected Legacy	Catherine George
A Deal with Demakis	Tara Pammi
The Ultimate Playboy	Maya Blake
Her Irresistible Protector	Michelle Douglas
The Maverick Millionaire	Alison Roberts
The Return of the Rebel	Jennifer Faye
The Tycoon and the Wedding Planner	Kandy Shepherd

HISTORICAL

A Lady of Notoriety	Diane Gaston
The Scarlet Gown	Sarah Mallory
Safe in the Earl's Arms	Liz Tyner
Betrayed, Betrothed and Bedded	Juliet Landon
Castle of the Wolf	Margaret Moore

MEDICAL

200 Harley Street: The Proud Italian	Alison Roberts
200 Harley Street: American Surgeon in London	Lynne Marshall
A Mother's Secret	Scarlet Wilson
Return of Dr Maguire	Judy Campbell
Saving His Little Miracle	Jennifer Taylor
Heatherdale's Shy Nurse	Abigail Gordon

Mills & Boon® Hardback

December 2014

ROMANCE

Taken Over by the Billionaire	Miranda Lee
Christmas in Da Conti's Bed	Sharon Kendrick
His for Revenge	Caitlin Crews
A Rule Worth Breaking	Maggie Cox
What The Greek Wants Most	Maya Blake
The Magnate's Manifesto	Jennifer Hayward
To Claim His Heir by Christmas	Victoria Parker
Heiress's Defiance	Lynn Raye Harris
Nine Month Countdown	Leah Ashton
Bridesmaid with Attitude	Christy McKellen
An Offer She Can't Refuse	Shoma Narayanan
Breaking the Boss's Rules	Nina Milne
Snowbound Surprise for the Billionaire	Michelle Douglas
Christmas Where They Belong	Marion Lennox
Meet Me Under the Mistletoe	Cara Colter
A Diamond in Her Stocking	Kandy Shepherd
Falling for Dr December	Susanne Hampton
Snowbound with the Surgeon	Annie Claydon

MEDICAL

Midwife's Christmas Proposal	Fiona McArthur
Midwife's Mistletoe Baby	Fiona McArthur
A Baby on Her Christmas List	Louisa George
A Family This Christmas	Sue MacKay

Mills & Boon® Large Print
December 2014

ROMANCE

HISTORICAL

MEDICAL

MILLS & BOON®

Why shop at millsandboon.co.uk?

Each year, thousands of romance readers find their perfect read at millsandboon.co.uk. That's because we're passionate about bringing you the very best romantic fiction. Here are some of the advantages of shopping at www.millsandboon.co.uk:

* **Get new books first**—you'll be able to buy your favourite books one month before they hit the shops

* **Get exclusive discounts**—you'll also be able to buy our specially created monthly collections, with up to 50% off the RRP

* **Find your favourite authors**—latest news, interviews and new releases for all your favourite authors and series on our website, plus ideas for what to try next

* **Join in**—once you've bought your favourite books, don't forget to register with us to rate, review and join in the discussions

Visit **www.millsandboon.co.uk**
for all this and more today!